IT'S COMPLICATED

Short stories about women, life and loss

Julia Graves

I am a woman undefined.
I am shy but I am brave,
I am strong but I c
            r
              u
                m
                  b
                    l
                      e
                        to your touch,
I find strength in time alone but I long to be near you,
and as I lose myself in you, so I find my way home.

Contents

Julia Graves

Twenty-Nine

So, I find myself semi-naked, your gloved hand on my breast. I can sense your boredom as you feel around mechanically, more through duty than expectation. It's hardly likely to be an issue, you think. I'm 29, after all, not 59.

"It's not unusual for girls your age to experience some knottiness," you say, smiling insincerely.

But then I tell you that my mum died at 29. Of breast cancer. I see your eyes flicker with excitement. This could be something, you think. And just as quickly, the flicker is gone. You damp it down. You smile reassuringly, tell me it's unlikely to be a problem. But you'll refer me to the hospital just the same. Just in case.

I wish I could have seen Dr Caspar like I usually do. But this was urgent. It's only a tiny lump, but a lump is a lump in my book. And whilst I want to ignore it, to pretend it's not there, I know I can't afford to do so. And so I made the appointment, ignoring the receptionist's pleas to wait until Dr Caspar was available and opting instead to see you today.

And I know, despite your reluctance, despite the hunch of your shoulders as you fill in the referral form, that this could be the first step in a chain of action that saves my life.

I tell nobody about my appointment at the hospital. Not Dad. Not Cara. Only you and the hospital referrals system know my little secret.

I never expected the appointment to come through so soon. At least they are taking my situation seriously, but somehow the implied urgency makes me even more anxious than I already was. I think back to your reluctance to act and it calms me.

Then I think of Cara, her little face smiling at me as I tucked her in last night. I dare not think what I would tell her, if...

But there's nothing to say, I tell myself. There will be nothing to say, no news to break, no battles to be fought until I have seen the consultant. I continue to walk, concentrating on putting one foot in front of the other, knowing that each step takes me closer to reality.

The hospital door swishes open, the lights flickering lazily as I approach. A cleaner drags a vacuum around the deserted reception area, ignoring me as I step over the cable, following the signs to the Kestrel Unit. There, a bored administrator sits behind another, smaller reception desk, but she doesn't leap to my assistance. I ding the bell in annoyance.

"All right," she says curtly. "I'll be with you in a minute."

I start to count the seconds in my head, but I get only to 29 before she passes me a clipboard with a couple of forms. "Medical history," she says, pointing at the first. "Family history," and she flicks to the second.

I take the clipboard and sit down, trying not to dwell on being cut off at 29. It's not a sign, I tell myself. It's just a coincidence.

The consultant is a small man with an exotic accent and an unpronounceable name. I spend the first couple of minutes trying to figure out where he is from as he runs through my answers to the questionnaires.

"Your maternal grandmuzzer," he says, tripping over the 'th'.

"Mmm?" I say.

"She died of...?"

I shrug. How can I explain that I don't know my own family history? That with Mum gone and Dad so ... fragile ... I have no-one left to ask. I was so young when it all happened, first Mum and then Grandma, leaving Dad and me to muddle on through.

"Not cancer?" he says.

I shrug again.

"Okay," he says, eyebrows raised in defeat. "You get undressed and I feel the breast." He waves a hand towards a scraggy curtain, which the nurse peels back with a swish, as if this were a game show and I the lucky contestant.

"Okay," I say, fighting back the giggles. It all seems so absurd, as if I will wake up any minute.

The pressure of his hand on my breast tells me I will not.

"Hmm," he says once he has finished. "I send you for an ultrasound, okay?"

"Okay," I say, my fears rising.

"It's probably nothing," he says. I hear the unspoken 'but', wait for it to be voiced but it doesn't come.

"Okay," I say again.

The nurse ushers me down the corridor to another waiting area. She hands over my file at the desk and smiles at me as she makes her way back again. I try to read her smile, but it is impossible. She has worked here too long, seen too many patients to give anything away.

I wait, watching as the only other patient snuggles up to her husband, who places a protective hand on her rounded stomach. I wonder why they are here on the graveyard shift, like me. I hope it is not bad news.

All at once, my fears for Cara assail me like a sledgehammer to the chest. Whatever would she do without me? I wonder, panic rising.

I am still fighting to regain control when my name is called by another, younger nurse. I take a deep breath and follow her through to another room, where again I am expected to disrobe in front of yet another man I do not know.

"Now then," he says, squeezing some gel from a bottle onto my breast. "This might be cold."

It is, but he's too late with his warning. Already a squeal of shock has escaped my mouth.

"So," he says, looking at my records. "You're 29?"

"Yes," I gasp.

"Well then," he says, picking up the ultrasound probe, "I'm sure you've nothing to worry about."

I count the seconds, holding my breath as he moves it across my breast.

Twenty-seven, twenty-eight, twenty-nine...

Julia Graves

Broken

"Stop!" The word is out of my mouth before I know it. Plump, round and deliciously unexpected. "Just stop!"

Stuart stares at me open-mouthed. He isn't used to me talking to him like this; he isn't used to me saying anything he doesn't want me to say. He slips off his coat and hangs it on the hook, taking his time before responding, but I'm not about to let him steal the moment. I've reached the point of no return. It's time to launch my attack.

"Stop lying to me!" I say. The look on his face changes from one of shock, of incredulity, to one I've never seen there before. A look of apprehension.

It doesn't last long. It takes just seconds for him to regain his composure. But I've seen through the crack.

"Lying?" he asks, looking hurt. Perhaps he really is shocked, I think, but not hurt. Not Stuart.

"There's no need to act offended," I say, my heart pounding.

How I need a brandy! I sat and contemplated the bottle, sorely tempted, but I knew that alcohol would dull my senses and I'd need to be sharp for this. I need to be razor-sharp.

"Don't act offended?" He puts his keys in the blue ceramic pot by the door and bends to unlace his shoes, which he places on the rack, stopping to tuck the laces inside. His self-control has gone into overdrive, but I know that he could snap at any minute.

"Where have you really been?" I ask, trying not to let my voice waver. Why am I doing this, I wonder, when I already know? But I need to hear it from his own lips. I need him to admit it.

"Does it matter?" he says, his voice taut.

I shrug. "I don't know. Does it?"

"And if I told you?" He stares at me hard, but he's wrong if he thinks I'm about to back down.

"Well, that depends," I say. "On whether you tell me the truth and on what the truth is." But now I'm the one who's lying. There is no going back.

"Hmm." He pushes his way past me into the kitchen, where he grabs a bottle of beer from the fridge. He heads towards the utensil drawer for the bottle-opener, but I block his way. He raises a hand and I brace myself for the blow, but it doesn't come. Instead, he laughs softly. "And you think I don't own you," he whispers, his bitter breath warm on my face.

The tears are quick to spring to my eyes and I curse myself for showing weakness.

"Well?" I follow him through to the living room where he rummages in another drawer, but I've hidden that bottle-opener too.

"You bitch!"

I quiver with a strange feeling of excitement as the bottle explodes against the wall, sending a shower of glass and cold lager spraying over the brown faux-leather sofa we once bought together. We ended up with his preferred fabric, of course, his preferred style. How I've grown to hate that sofa.

I close my eyes as a reflex against the flying glass, but I'm determined to stand my ground. When I look again, he's staring at me in confusion, no doubt wondering why I haven't scuttled off upstairs to lick my emotional wounds. But I know now that my wounds are the source of my strength, the source of my anger. And they will not heal until I've seen this through.

"I'll tell *you* then," I say slowly, "if you're not going to tell me."

He continues to stare at me, his eyes burning into mine, but still he says nothing.

"Theresa Riley."

He flinches when he hears her name and for a moment, I wonder whether he's going to deny it. Even though I've seen them together. Even though I followed them, knowing that he would never for one moment suspect any such thing. But, instead, he nods slowly. "And?"

"And what?"

He laughs unconvincingly. "So, you're my keeper now are you?"

I tilt my head on one side, feeling the bitterness well up, letting it build. "No," I say. "I'm your wife."

It's late when he finally leaves, a bag stuffed full of his best clothes under his arm. He says he'll be back in the morning, that he's just giving me the night to calm down, but we both know this is the end. Even so, I notice he takes his door keys, for all the good they'll do him. It's no exaggeration to say that I have the emergency locksmith on speed-dial. I pour myself that brandy, trying to stop my hand from shaking, and pick up the phone.

I don't have long to wait before Tim's van pulls up outside. I open the door and watch him stroll up the path.

It's a clear night and the stars are shining brightly, like fireworks lighting up the sky.

"So?" he says, stepping inside and setting his toolbox down. "You did it?"

"I did it," I say, a wave of giddiness sweeping over me.

He smiles as he bends to kiss me, barely even reacts to the smell of brandy, though I know he doesn't like it.

His lips are soft, his arms strong, his muscles firm beneath his t-shirt, but he holds me gently, stroking my hair with the very tips of his fingers as if scared he might break me. As if I wasn't already broken.

I want him to show me the new locks, to see him put them in so I can be sure that Stuart is really gone, but Tim shoos me away. "You don't need to worry about that," he tells me. "I'll take care of it. Trust me."

He's right. I must. Whatever he wants. Whatever he needs.

"I'll have a cup of tea," he says. "Strong, two sugars."

I nod and hurry to put the kettle on.

Darkness

This time of year is always the hardest for me, and this year more so than ever. It's not just that the nights are drawing in, or the darkness in the mornings. It's not just that the sun barely shows its face any more and the rain comes almost every day. It is all of these things and more. The echoes of the past chime in my mind like church bells, but there is no forgiveness, no redemption for me.

"Lisa!" The tutor's looking at me again with that expression on her face. I know she doesn't like me. She pretends to like me, but I can tell that she prefers the younger girls with their pretty, smiley faces, the way they hang off her every word.

It's not that I don't want to do well. I do. I completely understand how important it is for me to be able to stand on my own two feet now I'm back in my own place. But I never really learnt to do maths when I was at school and I never needed to know much about maths when I was at home with the twins.

"Of course you do!" Emily says, twirling her name badge. "If you have twins, you must have to double things all the time. Twice as much food, twice as much milk..." I know what she's trying to do. It's called contextualization. I read about it in a leaflet.

"No," I say. "I just did everything twice." I kick myself mentally for my use of the past tense, my first slip, but she doesn't seem to notice.

"Well, we all use maths all the time," she says, brightly. "Let's see, you probably set an alarm so you knew when to get up this morning."

She's right. I did have to set an alarm. I also had to take the right number of pills and check I had enough fuel in the car to get me here and back but I'm not going to tell her that.

I'm relieved when break-time comes around. "Ten minutes," Emily announces with a smile. "So that means we'll be back at...?" She looks around questioningly, but the tall skinny guy's already on his way to the coffee machine and the girl next to me is talking loudly about her son's birthday outing.

The guilt hits me like a shockwave.

"I'm sorry," I say, pushing my chair back abruptly and heading for the door. "I can't do this any more."

The car is still where I left it. Last week, I came back and it had rolled all the way down the hill to rest against an old VW. It was hard to tell whether it had done any damage; both cars were as beaten-up as each other. I left a note with my number, but I never heard anything. Even strangers whose cars I ram want nothing to do with me.

I get into the car and drive, not knowing where I'm going, or at least, that's what I tell myself. I've another two hours before my next appointment. Plenty of time to get my head back together.

It's only when I get there that I realise I knew where I was going all along. The wind has picked up and is whipping the clouds across the darkening sky. Fat drops of rain start to fall on the windscreen and I turn the wipers on to flick them away. Far below, I can hear the waves crashing onto the rocky shore. A seagull screams above, almost as if it is laughing. I shut my eyes and put my hands to my ears, trying to block out the memory, but, of course, it resides within me, and soon I can hold it back no more.

He was three when it happened. It was a gloomy, overcast day, just like today, but his smile was as bright as the sun. He wanted nothing more than an ice cream and a ride on a donkey.

"It's not a day for ice creams," I told him. What a fool I was!

"Ice cream, ice cream," he and Mandy started chanting together.

Impatiently, I bundled them into their pushchair and set off along the footpath, heading back over the clifftops towards the car park, head down against the wind.

I've been over it time and time again in my head, hundreds, no, thousands of times, but each time takes me further away from the truth.

Did the zip on Mandy's jacket really jam? Did Jack really throw sand in my face? Or are they false memories, planted to excuse myself for my inattention?

And then come the whys: why did my boss have to choose that moment to ring? Why did I turn my back on the twins, even for an instant? Why did I ignore Mandy's cries of "Mummy... Mummy...?"

I open the door and climb from the car, longing to feel the wind in my hair. It's then that I spot him: a young boy, splashing in the rock pools in his red wellington boots, fishing net in hand.

I step closer to the edge, peering down at him, my heart pounding as I watch him so close to the waves, and suddenly it's not him I see any more but Jack: Jack motionless on the rocky shore; Jack being carried into the ambulance; Jack lying lifeless on the hospital bed, while Mandy clung to my leg and cried for her brother who would never cry again.

I raise a hand and begin to wave and call. The boy looks up at me and my heart leaps. He has Jack's eyes. He has Jack's smile.

"Wait there!" I shout, crouching and starting to slither down the steep slope towards the shore.

This time, I won't let him down.

Stranded

The A-road is deserted when the car finally comes to a halt, slithering to a stop beside a snowbank. The windscreen wipers continue their battle against the elements, but all Jeannie can see is white, all around.

She says nothing as her son tries to restart the engine, again and again, until she can take no more.

"Please stop," she says, placing a hand gently on his arm. "Ron, it's no good."

He lets out a deep sigh and turns the key. The rhythmic swish of the wipers stops abruptly, leaving nothing but the howling of the wind and the pounding of snow on the windscreen.

"I'm sure I put a can in the boot," he says, making to throw the door open for the third time, but Jeannie puts a hand on his arm to stop him.

"You didn't," she says.

"Well you didn't either," he says. "Did you?"

Jeannie opens her mouth to object, but she sees the flash of anger in his eyes and bites her tongue. If the years have taught her one thing, it's to pick her battles carefully. But she wonders now whether getting a mobile phone is one battle she should have fought harder.

"Oh well," she sighs. "It's not the end of the world."

He turns to look at her and she braces herself, but to her surprise he just reaches into the back of the car.

"Here," he says, passing her a flask of tea and unfolding a map on the dashboard.

It's not a lot but it's enough to bring a tear to her eye. It's the second time in two days he's surprised her. Maybe this time things will be different, she thinks. Maybe he really has learnt from his mistakes.

She pours the hot, brown liquid from the flask into the tall, plastic cup, watching as the steam forms a cloud on the windscreen.

"Here," she says, passing the cup to Ron, but he waves it away. "Busy, Mother," he says, his finger tracing a route across the map. After a few minutes, he puts it away and sits drumming his thumbs on the steering wheel.

"Well?" she asks.

"Well what?"

"Well, what are we going to do now?"

"OK," he says, glaring at her. "You've made your point."

It's then she decides to be quiet. It's not like they have many options. With or without the cast on her leg, she wouldn't get far in this snow and Ron's not in the mood to play the hero. It's enough that he agreed to bring her in the first place. She couldn't have managed the clutch in her car, and she knows better than to ask to borrow his automatic.

It's not long before Ron's snoring, his breath coming in great bursts that reverberate through the vehicle.

Jeannie wishes sleep came so easily to her. It used to, once upon a time, but as age has crept up on her, sleep has fled. She closes her eyes and tries to clear her mind, feeling the cold probing at her brain even as it steals the feeling from her fingers and toes. Resignedly, she hunkers down in her seat and waits for morning to come.

She's woken, disorientated, by a tapping on the window. At first, she wonders whether it's just a tree branch blowing against the windscreen, but there's a bright light shining and as her eyes adjust, she sees a man's face peering in, woolly hat pulled down over thick ginger hair.

She reaches for the handle and winds the window down, shivering as the cold wind rushes in.

"Are you all right, love?" the man says.

She forces a smile. "Fine, thank you," she says politely, though her head feels heavy. "Bit cold."

The man pats the handle of his shovel. "Dig you out?" he says.

"Thanks," she says with a shrug, "but we're out of fuel."

"We?" he puts his head on one side, eyebrow raised.

"Me and my son." She glances across to the driver's seat, only now registering that Ron's not there. "He was right here," she says, patting the seat. "Must have wandered off to look for fuel."

"Right you are," the farmer says. "Well, I'll just start digging, shall I?"

He's done in no more than half an hour.

"I'd offer you a cup of tea," she says raising the empty flask, "but I've drunk it all."

He laughs. "I'll be heading off then," he says, pointing to his tractor. "Sure you don't want a lift anywhere?"

Jeannie hesitates. Much as she doesn't fancy being left out on the road alone, it's what Ron would expect. "I'd better wait here," she says, finally.

"Well, okay then."

She watches as he swings himself up into the cab before closing her eyes again. She's on the verge of drifting back to sleep when there comes another tap at the window.

"Blanket," he says, passing one through to her.

"Oh no, really," she says. "You mustn't..."

"Look," he says with a smile. "If you won't come with me, you can at least take my old blanket."

"But-"

"But nothing. A soul could perish out here on a night like this."

The sun is creeping over the horizon when she next wakes. There's still no sign of Ron, just snowy white fields and the shape of the road snaking through the valley. She throws the door open and pulls herself up onto her good leg, stretching cramped muscles.

It's not long before the tractor rumbles back past. "You still here?" the farmer says, a look of concern on his face.

"Your blanket," she says, holding it out to him. "Thank you."

He frowns, eyebrows deeply furrowed. "Your son?"

"Not back yet," she says. "He must have decided to stay over in town."

He nods, weighing the blanket in his hands. "Look," he says. "You must be famished. At least come back to the farmhouse. I'll make you some tea, spot of breakfast. You'll be more comfortable there."

She chews her lip for a moment, thinking. "I don't' know. My son-"

"Look," he says. "I won't take no for an answer." But the look on his face is kindly.

She shrugs. "Just for a short while then."

Jeannie has barely got settled by the fire with a cup of tea when there's a knock on the door. She tenses, but the farmer smiles reassuringly.

"You stay here," he says.

Jeannie cranes her neck, trying to see who's there, but he's pulled the kitchen door to behind him and she can only see a sliver of white through the crack.

"What's all this then?" the visitor says in a low voice.

"Think you'd better see for yourself. She says her son brought her out here and went off looking for fuel, but..." The farmer hesitates. "I don't know."

Jeannie frowns.

"She'd been there a while," he says, "so it's hard to say for sure. Looked like there might have been someone with her, but no tracks heading to town. Maybe he went the wrong way."

It's not the farmer but a woman who first appears at the kitchen door. Jeannie's surprised to see she's wearing a police uniform. The farmer follows, a sheepish look on his face.

"There's no need to worry yourselves," Jeannie says.

"I know." The policewoman perches beside her, pulling out her mobile phone. "But it's been a devil of a night. We need to make sure your son's ok."

Ron. Jeannie swallows. She'd never even contemplated that something might have happened to him.

"What's his number, love?" the policewoman asks gently.

"Ron? He doesn't have a mobile."

"Home phone then?"

Jeannie frowns. "There's no point calling. There's no-one there."

"Humour me."

Reluctantly, Jeannie gives the number, watching as the policewoman dials. It rings once, twice, three times. Then finally, unexpectedly, it's answered.

"Hello?" Ron's voice is tinny through the phone's speaker.

"Hello," the policewoman says. "Mr Morris? This is PC Muriel Higgins-"

"It's Mum, isn't it?"

"That's right." She glances at Jeannie and smiles.

"Tell me."

"She was found in your car on the A86 not long ago."

"A86?"

"That's right."

"In my car?" Ron goes quiet, just for a moment. "I blame myself," he says slowly.

"Blame yourself, sir?"

"If I hadn't left my keys lying about... If I'd taken the last time as a warning." Jeannie frowns. She opens her mouth to protest, but he's still talking. "But you know, you can't watch over them all the time."

PC Higgins turns away, lowering her voice. "It's not the first time then?"

She's holding the phone to her ear now and Jeannie can't make out Ron's reply.

"Aye, she's had quite the rough night."

For a few moments, the line is silent before the low hum of Ron's reply comes through.

The policewoman looks surprised. "Dead?" she says. "She's not-"

Without warning, Jeannie shoots out a hand and grabs the phone, hitting the button to end the call. The policewoman opens her mouth in surprise, but Jeannie doesn't wait for her speak.

"You've got to help me," she says.

Julia Graves

Bearing the Load

It was dark when the young man stepped out of the pub, his teammates' congratulations ringing in his ears. He stopped to pull his collar up against the cold and bent to light a cigarette.

He didn't see the man hiding behind the skip. He didn't see the plank clutched in his hand, riddled with nails. He didn't see the blow coming, so he did nothing to protect himself.

An instant later, he was laid out cold.

Blood trickled from his right eye, red against the snow.

Grandad Jim always used to say, "You won't get anywhere in life without trying, young lady." Always with the 'young lady'. Always telling me what to do and what not to do and that I needed to raise my game.

But what did he know about it? He was seventy if he was a day, blind in one eye, with a pronounced limp. He never got out of his chair except when he needed to visit the bathroom. But that didn't stop him nagging on at me.

If I'm honest, I was always a little scared of Grandad Jim. He never took me out for ice cream like my Grandad Rex, never came to see me in a school play or took me to the beach. He just sat in his chair and bossed me and Mum around, demanding cups of tea and bacon sandwiches, which he chewed horribly with his oversized dentures.

So, it was something of a relief when I left home to go to university and was spared the weekly visits to his flat.

When I returned for Christmas, he was gone, victim of a heart attack. I can't say I was all that sorry. Now we could enjoy Christmas, just the three of us, without Grandad Jim leering at me from his chair in the corner.

To my surprise, Mum wasn't taking it so well. If I'd expected relief at having regained her freedom, I was mistaken. Her red-rimmed eyes told another story.

"He was her father," Dad murmured to me as Mum bent tearfully over Grandad's open coffin. "Be gentle with her."

We were in the car returning home when Mum asked me to be one of the pallbearers.

"I can't do that!" I said.

"Why not?" Mum twisted round in her seat to stare at me. "Because you're a girl?" She frowned. "We brought you up to know better than that."

And the truth was that they did. For all his faults, Grandad Jim had never believed there was anything I couldn't do if I tried hard enough. But still, the thought of carrying his coffin, his bony head so close to mine, made me shudder.

"Please," Mum said, tears welling in her eyes. How could I say no?

And so it was arranged. The other pallbearers were to be my Uncle James, and my cousins, George and Ruth, who flew in from Scotland the night before the funeral. I hadn't seen them for years, but they hadn't changed a bit.

"Katie." George nodded to me as he heaved their bags out of the taxi.

"Hi Katie." Ruth gave me a smile as tight as her chignon.

Uncle James wasn't so reticent. No sooner was he through the door than he scooped me up in his arms and planted a kiss on top of my head. "Long time no see, Number One Niece," he said.

"I'm your *only* niece," I said, rolling my eyes, but I couldn't help but smile.

"Ah, that'll be why, then," he said with a wink as he followed Mum through to the kitchen.

George, Ruth and I stood in the hallway looking awkwardly at one another.

"I suppose we could go to the pub," I said.

"Top idea." George said, looking relieved at the opportunity to escape the dull task of finalising the funeral arrangements. "Let's go."

The Rose and Crown was a traditional pub, dark and dingy with a low ceiling. The Christmas tree twinkled incongruously in the corner.

"Grandad must have loved it in here," Ruth said, taking a sip of her drink.

"Grandad?" I said, surprised.

"Yes, he loved a pint, didn't he?"

I shrugged. "Well, if you say so..."

"Oh yes," George said. "Well, he was a darts champion, after all."

"Grandad?" I said again, almost spitting out my beer in surprise. "Grandad Jim?"

"Yes." Ruth frowned at me. "Don't say you didn't know."

"I didn't. I'd no idea."

"Well, I suppose," George said, "maybe he didn't like to talk about it, after... you know."

"After what?"

"George!" Ruth shot him a warning glance.

"No," I said, holding up a hand to stop her. "I'd like to know."

It was 1975 when it happened. Mum was just 8 years old and had recently been adopted.

"Adopted?" I said, horrified.

"You see?" Ruth said, glaring at George. "She didn't know."

But it was too late then. George had started telling me the tale and I wasn't going to let him stop.

"Her birth parents were both heavy drinkers," he said. "Her father was violent, her mother neglectful. But when their daughter was taken from them, they didn't want to let her go."

"It was after a darts match. Grandad had won. He stayed and had a drink with his teammates, then set off to walk home. And that's when it happened."

I sat, appalled as he told me about the attack.

"And so, it was him?" I said, horrified. "Mum's father."

"Grandad Jim was your mum's father," Ruth said. "Why do you think she never told you she was adopted?"

I nodded slowly, trying to understand.

"Grandad didn't like to talk about what happened," George said. "But he never blamed your mum."

"He couldn't play darts any more after that, of course," Ruth said, quietly. "Couldn't do much of anything, really." She shook her head. "Shame."

And so, I found myself lined up beside the coffin, awaiting the instruction to lift. How could I have been so wrong about the man, I asked myself. How could I not have known what he had done for my mother - and in so doing, for me?

I had ridden quietly in the funeral car, squeezing my mother's hand as she sobbed gently, not revealing to her what I had learned. I knew that, one day, the time would come.

For now, she needed me to be there for her, to help her carry the weight of the past.

Julia Graves

Blood and Betrayal

I knew as soon as I got home that something wasn't right. It's hard to explain, but when you've lived in a place for 20 years, you just know when somebody else has been there.

It's not like the door was hanging off its hinges or the hall was a mess. At first, I wondered whether I was going mad, but I could sense that something was wrong. I wasn't sure whether I should go on in, or whether I should step outside and call the police, or at least my daughter, Daisy, but what would I say? I've got home and the place feels different? No. I shook myself. They would think I was crazy, and who was to say that I wasn't? But nevertheless, I grabbed an umbrella from the coat-stand, holding it out in front of me like a truncheon before heading through to the kitchen.

I jumped as I heard the clatter of plastic on plastic, but it was just the cat flap. Topsy wandered through, haughty as ever. I never liked the animal, but Daisy insisted that I needed a presence around the house after her father passed on, something to keep me company, and at least she doesn't demand much attention.

I turned and made my way through to the living room. It was then I saw that the French doors were standing ajar, the wood cracked and splintered where someone had forced their way in. I gasped and looked around me wildly, but there was no sign of the intruder. Still, I headed back outside in haste: who knew whether he was still inside? Hands shaking, I pulled out my phone and dialled Daisy's number.

"Daisy, I-"

"Mum," she said. "What's wrong? Has something happened?"

I hadn't realised that I'd sounded so shaken. "I'm fine, darling," I said, trying to breathe deeply. "I just... I've had a little bit of a shock... It looks like I've been burgled."

"Burgled?"

"Really, I'm fine, darling. It doesn't like they took anything much but I'd just... I'd appreciate some company."

My voice tailed off as I realised how weak that sounded.

"If you've got the time, of course," I said. "I mean, I'll just get Ted from next door to come round if not."

"Of course I'll come!" she said. "Hold tight. I'll be there in five."

Hold tight to what? I wondered as I stared at the screen of my phone, her smiling face replaced by a series of icons for such frivolities as online Scrabble. Daisy had installed them before gifting the phone to me, my turn to benefit from her hand-me-downs for a change.

"Are you all right there, Daphne?"

I looked up in surprise at the sound of Ted's voice.

"Why, yes, thank you Ted," I said, but the emotion of the moment overtook me and to my surprise I found myself sobbing into my handkerchief.

"Whatever is it, Daphne?" he said in his heavy West Country accent, hovering awkwardly, looking very much out of his depth.

"I - oh, you're going to think I'm terribly silly," I said, wiping away my tears. "It's just that ... well, I seem to have suffered a break-in."

"A break-in!" Ted looked horrified. "Well then, we'd best call the police, sharpish."

"Yes, I suppose, but it's not clear yet what was taken."

Ted looked set to argue but his words were drowned out by a screech of tyres. We both looked towards the end of the road, where Daisy's car had turned the corner at high speed. She pulled up next to the kerb and jumped out, quick sharp, slamming the door behind her.

"Mum! Thank goodness you're ok!" she said, rushing to my side. I could tell she must have left home in a hurry as her hair was a mess and she had forgotten to put her second earring in. I felt a rush of warmth towards her for responding so quickly in my hour of need.

"Yes, yes, I'm ok," I said. "I was at choir practice-"

"I know, but the shock of it!" She nodded curtly at Ted and steered me towards the front door. "We must get you a hot drink and then get some of your things together."

"Why on earth would we do that?"

"I was just telling your mother to call the police," Ted shouted after us. "Can't be letting scoundrels get away with breaking in, even if they didn't take nothing."

"Oh no, we won't need to do that, will we, Mum?" she said, following me through the door and shutting it firmly behind us. "Now then, you go and get yourself sat down and I'll pack you a case."

"Pack me a case? Whatever for?"

"You're not staying here after this."

"But Daisy, where would I go?"

"You can come and stay with me."

"Oh Daisy, really, it's not necessary," I said. "Anyway, look, I'm not sure I'm happy with you going up there by yourself. They might still be here."

Daisy's laugh seemed a little strained. Presumably she was worried about the possibility as well, but she couldn't show it. "I'm sure they're long gone," she said. "Probably just kids."

"I don't know, Daisy."

"Well, look, if you feel happier, you come up with me. You can pack your own case."

I frowned, wondering when she would finally get the message. "Daisy," I said. "I've told you time and again, I am not leaving this house. This is where your father lived and died. Why would I want to be anywhere else?"

"But it's so big, Mum. Surely you'd be happy somewhere a bit more ... manageable." She shook her head. "Anyway, no need to worry about that right now. All we're talking is a few days at my place. I'm not asking you again."

"Then don't."

"What does that mean?"

I sighed. "Look, Daisy, I think perhaps you coming over was a mistake. I'm fine. I'm just tired and emotional. I'm sure you're right and they're long gone. I'll just get Ted to come and board the door up and-"

"I'm not sure I want that man hanging around here."

"Ted?"

"Yes. I saw the way he looked at you."

"Ted?" I repeated, incredulous.

"Look, Mum, do you want my help or not?" she said, a sullen look on her face.

I took a deep breath. "Daisy," I said as gently as I could. "I know you're trying to help, but really, I'm fine. I think perhaps you should just leave."

"Leave?"

I nodded.

"Well, thanks'd be a fine thing," she said, picking up her handbag and heading for the door. "Honestly, mother, ring me when you come to your senses and I'll come back and get you. Any time." And with that, she breezed out, slamming the door behind her.

Two hours later, Ted had finished boarding up the doors and packed up his things ready to go. He had insisted on checking the first floor and reported back with a grin that it was 'all clear,' just like one of the cops in the crime shows he so likes watching on TV.

"Odd though," he said, shaking his head. "If I didn't know better, I'd swear those doors had been forced from the inside."

I raised my eyebrows at him, and he shrugged and took his leave. "I'm just glad you're all right, Daphne," he said. "Call me if you need anything."

I relaxed as I shut the door behind him. It had been an emotionally exhausting day, so even though I'd barely eaten, I decided to turn in for the night.

I almost didn't see it, the tiny earring on the floor in the ensuite, but it caught the light in just such a way that it glinted at me brightly.

Ruby red. The colour of blood and betrayal.

I picked it up and squeezed my hand shut around it, feeling it dig into my palm, the pain as sharp and bright as a dagger to my chest.

Road Rage

The rain stings my face as I hurry along the slick pavement, blown on an icy wind. Sirens howl in the distance, cutting through the low drone of engines as cars queue to get into the town centre. I think of my own car, abandoned on a suburban street under the gaze of a disapproving homeowner. But what choice did I have?

I up my pace, conscious of just how late for work I already am.

To think I left home in such buoyant mood! It's not that there's anything I'm particularly looking forward to today; not work-wise at least. But my new coat came yesterday, and I can't wait to show it off to Tracy. Then last night I found an old photo of the two of us at the Christmas party, must have been twenty years ago now, and it made me smile. We've both got really stupid perms and the *jumpers*! Hard to believe just how much fashions have changed. I just know she'll burst into hoots of laughter when she sees her big glasses and bigger hair, and the way she's got her arms wrapped around old George McKearney.

He was all right, was George. Straight as an arrow and twice as direct, but he was on our side. Not like the new management, always looking to get more out of us for less. Especially Colin. Creepy Colin we call him. Probably on the phone to HR right now to complain that I'm late.

It's not like it's even my fault. I got up dead on time, got showered and dressed, didn't even stop for breakfast. Yes, I had to deice the car, but I'd left time, really I had, plus a bit extra on account of the conditions. Shame not everyone's as forward thinking. They drive too fast, pure and simple. Selfish it is. They should know that stretch of road's treacherous; there are accidents often enough. But people forget, or they don't care. And then it's people like me who suffer, sitting in queues for hours.

Multiple vehicle collision they said on the radio. Expect delays. Perhaps I should have stopped then and phoned Colin, but once you leave the queue you never get back in again. More selfishness. As if it's going to hurt to let one more car join the queue, but people don't think like that, do they?

The road was only closed for half a mile or so; it wasn't much of a diversion, but most people have no idea how to drive on single track roads. There's no co-operation, no forethought. It's like it's a competition to see who can be the most selfish. But whose idea it was to bring a ten-tonne truck down there, I'll never know!

Still, I made it through in the end. Course, by then it was the heart of the rush hour and the queues in town were almost as bad as the ones I'd just battled my way through. I got close enough to be able to walk the rest of the way and that was good enough for me. Been in the car almost two hours as it is; I couldn't bear to spend another minute battling the traffic. Just a shame that the heavens chose that moment to open, spilling their contents all over my new woollen coat. I can't wait to show it off to Tracy. Soggy or not, it's a classy bit of gear.

I reach the office building and pause briefly in the lobby, trying to compose myself. I pull my collar up to show my new coat off to best effect and head down the corridor, doing my best catwalk strut to get myself in the mood.

I pull open the door to the office, smile wide upon my face, expecting Tracy to be there at her desk by the door, but her chair is empty, her computer screen blank.

"Suzanne." Colin's voice makes me jump and I push my collar down self-consciously, realising he may be wondering why I'm so late, why I didn't so much as call.

"Sorry, Colin," I say, rearranging my face to look contrite. "The traffic's awful out there. There's been a terrible accident."

There is stony silence for just the briefest of moments before someone begins to cry, deep, throaty sobs echoing around the office. I look around, suddenly aware of the sea of bleak faces staring at me.

"Suzanne," Colin says again, more softly this time.

I look back at Tracy's empty desk, then with mounting horror at Colin's hand, which he has reached out to place on my arm.

He opens his mouth and closes it a couple of times before, finally, a word escapes. "It's…"

And already I know what it is, I know who it is, but I don't want to know, I don't want him to finish that sentence, I just want Tracy to be here with me now, laughing at the stupid photo and swooning over my coat and making faces behind Colin's stupid, uptight back.

"It's..."

And still he can't say her name and I don't want him to say it, but someone has to.

"Tracy," I say. And then the tears start to fall as pictures of her dance before my eyes and I whisper it like a prayer. "Tracy."

The Liar

It's only a small lie. "I thought I'd better come straight home," he says, sitting down beside me, "so I didn't keep my sugar waiting." The word 'again' hangs in the air, unspoken. "I didn't stop to talk to anyone."

That's when I know he's lying. His car isn't flashy, but I know it when I see it. And I saw it tonight, parked up by the side of the road, with its lights off.

I didn't think much of it at the time. We live out of town; it's hard to get about if you don't have transport of your own. So, there's nothing odd about Danny giving a friend a lift. He doesn't tell me everything; why should he? *But why lie?*

"Oh really," I say, the slightest edge of sarcasm to my voice, but if he recognises it, he shows no sign.

I take a deep breath, then let it out slowly. "I've, er, got something to tell you," I say, my hand moving protectively to my stomach.

"Mmm?" he says, tapping away at his phone.

I hesitate. My mind drifts back, unbidden, to a time just after we met.

"The key to telling a convincing lie," he told me, "is in sticking as close to the truth as possible." I laughed then, feeling the frisson of excitement at living dangerously, even though I knew we'd never get caught. He never had before.

"You must be mad," my brother said when I told him we were moving in together. "He can't be trusted, he's proved that."

"What do you mean?" I said.

Frank looked me hard in the eye. "He cheated on Laura," he said. "What makes you think he won't do the same to you?"

But he hasn't. I mean, I've never had reason to suspect him. Not really.

I think back to a journey home last week, remember smiling at the sight of his car parked outside the bar where he works, at knowing he was nearby.

"I saw your car tonight," I said when he came in.

"Where?" he asked, the question spoken too quickly.

"Outside Roscoe's, of course." I laughed. "Where do you think I saw it?"

Is it my imagination, or did he relax then? I didn't notice at the time but now I think back... No, I tell myself. You're just paranoid. It's the hormones. And yet... Yesterday he arrived home late. Very late.

"Sorry, babe," he said this morning. "I got talking to the boss about promotions."

"It's all right," I said, swallowing my annoyance. "I was worried about you, that's all."

It's true. I was worried. And now, mind working overtime, I'm more worried than ever.

"D'you still love me?" I say, leaning in for a kiss.

"Course I do," he says, eyes not leaving his phone.

"Good," I say, but I feel the tears start to burn.

"Babe." He looks up at me, eyebrows furrowed. "What's wrong?"

I take a deep breath, try to find the words to tell him, but they don't come.

"It's nothing," I lie.

Julia Graves

After Daniel

Daniel was such a sweet boy. On his first day at the nursery, when the other children were jostling for position, squabbling over the Duplo blocks and the crayons, Daniel hung back, watching, a smile on his face.

On his fourth birthday, when Amelia Jacobsen brought him a bag of sweets, he insisted on sharing them with the other children, even though his mother, Clara, had little money to spare for such treats. He was kind, generous, open-hearted, everyone's favourite, even though we weren't supposed to have favourites and tried hard not to show it. Which is why it was all the more shocking when he disappeared.

I first heard about it from a stranger. Daniel hadn't arrived at nursery that morning, and though we'd tried to contact his mother, she hadn't answered the phone or returned our calls. He probably just had a sniffle, we'd told ourselves. Hayley Cole had been sniffling the day before and had been kept at home that day. It had likely just hit Daniel harder, faster, what with him being such a slight boy. And no doubt Clara had forgotten to call us, caught up in trying to juggle a sick child, looking after her frail, elderly father and her part-time job at the local supermarket. And so, when the phone rang just after lunch and the caller said she was ringing about Daniel, it seemed likely she was phoning to pass on a message.

"How is he?" I said, trying to peel a small child from my ankles.

"You mean you haven't heard?" she said.

"Heard what?"

"He's missing," she said, and though she tried to sound downbeat, I could hear the excitement in her voice. "Not been seen since last night."

"What do you mean, he's missing?" I said and then, "Who is this?"

"Jane Tillerson, Waverley News."

A journalist? My heart leapt into my mouth. I'd already said too much, even admitting I knew the child, but more importantly, if the local newspaper was involved, it had to be serious. I ended the call and dialled Clara's number again, needing to hear it from her. Still she didn't answer.

"Lisa, can you cope without me for half an hour?" I asked my colleague, trying to keep the anxiety from my voice, not wanting to upset the other children.

She frowned at me, but she could tell it was serious. "Sure," she said, keeping her voice bright. "Kids, gather round. We're going to have story-time early today."

I smiled my thanks before grabbing my bag from the staff room and scooting out to the car.

The door to Daniel's house was open when I got there, which struck me as unusual. It was a small terraced house, the front garden neat but functional, the paint starting to peel from the windowsills. Somewhere nearby a dog was crying.

"Hello?" I called, knocking gently at the open door before stepping inside. "Clara?"

There was no reply, but as I pushed open the kitchen door, I could hear her sobbing at the table. "Clara," I said, racing over to her side. "It's true then."

She looked up at me, tears streaking her cheeks and nodded. "He's gone! Taken! Or..." She paused, choking back the tears, then shook her head. "But he's never run away before."

"You've spoken to the police, of course."

"Yes." She sniffed, dabbing at her face with a well-used tissue. "They've just left."

"All of them?" I was shocked. Surely they shouldn't have left her alone. "No family liaison officer?"

"No. I..." Again, a sob racked her chest and the tears started to slide down her cheeks. "I told them to go. I said I could cope on my own. I just want them to be out there finding him."

"But you can't cope, can you?"

She shook her head, eyes cast down at the table. I sat down beside her and placed my hand over hers. "Is there somewhere you can go? Someone I can call?"

"I just want to be here," she said, "in case..."

"In case he comes back." I nodded. "Maybe you could get a friend to come over. To wait with you."

"No," she said. "I don't... I don't know who I'd ask." She paused. "You'll wait with me though," she said, her eyes not leaving mine. "Won't you?"

I thought of Lisa, alone with all those children to look after. I needed to get back. But Clara looked so desperate. How could I leave her?

"Of course," I said.

It didn't take long for them to find him. I was only on my third cup of tea when the policewoman and her partner came to the door.

"Hello," I said, ushering them in.

"And you are?" She eyed me suspiciously.

"Jackie Trimble. I'm... a friend of Clara's," I said, not altogether truthfully.

"I see."

"She's in the kitchen."

I followed them through, watching as the policewoman took a seat opposite Clara, the grim-faced male officer hovering by the door.

"There's no easy way of saying this," the policewoman said, lowering her eyes to the table. Time seemed to stretch out before us, elongated, before she spoke again, but I already knew what she was going to say. "We've found a body."

Clara's hand shot to her mouth and the sound that came out was inhuman, all her pain, all her fear, all her guilt and rage distilled into that one sound as she rocked herself backwards and forwards, her face twisted in a torment of agony.

"We'll need you to make an identification," the policewoman said. "When you're ready." She reached out a hand to comfort Clara, but it was no good. Clara was in a world of her own, a world of pain and shock and anger.

"You don't need to wait," I told her, feeling for poor Clara, having to live out her worst nightmare in front of strangers. "We'll be fine." I tried to smile my thanks, but the tears were coursing down my cheeks too.

"Oh! Well..." She looked doubtfully from me to Clara and back again, but nevertheless, she stood to leave. "Okay. We'll wait outside," she said, nodding. "We'll let you know when everything's ready."

She paused on her way to the door and, looking back over her shoulder, added, "I'm very sorry," but it made no difference. She couldn't bring Daniel back. There was nothing anyone could do for him now, and nothing that could lessen the pain. Hope had been abandoned.

All that was left to do was wait.

The mortuary was nothing like I expected. On TV, they are all stainless steel, white sheets, grim-faced mortuary attendants and frosty cadavers. Yet here, I found myself in a tastefully decorated room, a heavy curtain drawn across the viewing window as the coroner explained to us what we could expect to see. Daniel had been beaten; his face would be bruised. He would be dressed so we would be spared the worst of his injuries. Clara nodded as the process was explained to her, but her eyes were haunted and she sat still, her eyelids heavy, her face drawn.

When the curtain was finally pulled back, there lay Daniel, his head resting on a pillow as if he were asleep, though it was clear from the pallor of his skin that he was gone. He looked almost peaceful, despite the angry purple bruise across his cheek. He was neatly dressed in a red tracksuit I'd never seen before. I briefly wondered whether it was his or something the staff had found for him, but I swallowed the question. What did it matter?

I tried to take a step back, to let Clara grieve in peace, but she clung onto me, pulling me over towards the window, her eyes not leaving his face all the while.

"Daniel," she moaned. "My sweet, sweet, Daniel. I'm so sorry, my angel. I'm so, so, sorry." It was almost more than I could bear.

We stayed an hour or so until, in spite of the rush of emotion of the day, my eyelids threatened to close. I offered for Clara to come home with me, but was relieved when she declined, saying she would sooner go to her father's house. I drove her there in silence and before she got out of the car she paused and took my hand.

"Thank you, Jackie," she said. "Thank you." I nodded but couldn't find the words to reply.

I sat there for long minutes after she let herself into the house, watching as the lights went on and then off again. I breathed in the night air and thanked the Lord for granting me this day, this hour, this minute of life. Then I put the car in gear and set off home.

I stayed in bed the next day, and the day after that, not answering the door, ignoring the phone until it ran out of charge. By Friday, I felt able to face the world but not my job, not the children. I plugged in the phone and dialled work.

"Good to hear from you," my boss said, her tone indicating that it was anything but.

"I'm sorry, Miranda," I said. "I-" But the words stuck in my throat.

"It's been a tough week for everyone," she said, her voice softening. "I know that. But we can't ignore what you did on Tuesday."

"What I did?"

"You breached our trust, Jackie. You abandoned your post, leaving vulnerable children without adequate care. You jeopardised the very future of our business."

"I went to look after Daniel's mother!"

"I know. And it was very noble of you. But it wasn't your job."

I was trembling by the time I hung up the phone. My mind was in bits, my thoughts whirling, snippets of our conversation caught up in the maelstrom: disciplinary action, suspension, representation, dismissal. And yet none of it mattered any more. I had loved my job. I had studied hard and scrapped harder to get that job but deep down I knew that it was over. There was no way I could go back now. Not after Daniel.

I didn't attend the dismissal hearing. The outcome was both certain and necessary.

"I'm sorry," Miranda said when she came to hand me my P45 and my personal effects. "If there was any other way..."

I didn't invite her in and I didn't try to defend myself.

There was nothing left to say.

I have asked myself, time and again, over the months and the years, whether I could have done things differently. Is it true, as I insisted at the time, that I would have done the same for any child? Or was it my particular affection for Daniel that made me act the way I did?

Sometimes I see Clara out and about in town. She keeps her head down and passes by on the other side of the street, never meeting my eye. Secretly, I am glad not to have to find the words to say, knowing that they can never ease her pain. Some mothers grow in strength when they lose a child, their rage lending them a power and presence they never knew they possessed, but not Clara. She has been nothing but diminished by Daniel's loss.

They never found the person who took him. They suspect Daniel left the house of his own accord, although quite why, nobody knows. Sometimes there are no answers, only more questions.

Exposure

It's the coldness of the church that is the biggest shock. Many things are familiar: the wooden pews, the heavy scent of polish in the air, the thin light filtering through the stained-glass windows, the hushed way of talking that people adopt in churches even on happier occasions.

All this takes me back to my childhood, when my parents would drag my sister and me along to the Sunday service at our parish church. The sermons were so dull we couldn't wait to be excused to run, whispering and giggling with our friends to our respective meeting rooms.

I bite down on the thought, tasting its bitterness in my mouth.

There's no giggling today, though there is plenty of whispering, people shuffling in their seats as they make room for friends and acquaintances.

I look around, wishing I'd accepted the offer of a lift from the office. The thought of having to listen to the salesgirls' chatter all the way here was more than I could bear but now, sitting here alone, I feel awkward and exposed.

I arrived early and chose my seat carefully: at the far end of the row, almost halfway back, at a respectful distance from the grieving family. The others came later and took their seats on the far side of the church. I glance over but they don't see me. I sigh and turn my attention back to the front of the church.

A huge photograph of Linda looms over the closed casket. I try not to think about what lies within.

I'm still staring at the photograph when an old man shuffles his way along the bench to sit down beside me. I bend my head to feign prayer, but I can feel his eyes upon me. When I look up, sure enough, he reaches out a hand in greeting.

"Tom," he says, his gaze unfaltering. "And you are?"

"Meg."

He nods as if that means something to him, though I know it can't. Linda and I may have shared an office, but that was all we shared. "Ruth will be glad you came."

I frown and follow his gaze to the door, where a thin girl is deep in conversation with the vicar.

"And how did you know Linda?" I say.

He laughs. "Everyone knows Linda."

I smile, though I've no idea what he means. I open my mouth to press him further, but the organ has started to play and the vicar begins making his way down the aisle. I close it again and join the rest of the congregation in standing.

I glance at my watch. Bang on time. With luck, I'll make it back to the office before the sandwich van closes.

Ruth is standing by the door as we leave, shaking hands with each person who passes, repeating the invitation to join the family at Linda's house. Her eyes look tired and red, but she seems genuine, nonetheless.

I have a smile and an apology on my lips but when I reach the front of the queue, I'm taken by surprise.

"And you must be Meg," she says.

"Yes. How-?"

"Well, you absolutely must join us for the wake."

"Oh, I-"

"Well, of course she's joining us," Tom cuts in from behind me.

"I-"

"I'm so glad," Ruth says, bending to hug me. "There's something Mum would have wanted you to have."

"Really?" I swallow and fix a weak smile on my face. "Well, in that case..."

"Come on then," Tom says, taking my arm. "It's not far, but these old legs won't carry me there on my own."

I glance over at my boss, who is staring at me in surprise, and shrug. I guess it doesn't have to be for long.

Linda's house is different from how I'd imagined, to the extent that I ever gave it any thought at all. The front room is decorated in a pink, floral print, with double doors that open out onto a well-tended garden at the back.

"Beautiful," I find myself murmuring.

"Ah, yes, she had green fingers all right," Tom says, settling himself onto the sofa. He pats the cushion next to him. I smile and take a seat.

The scent of coffee drifting through from the kitchen nudges at my memory. I can almost see Linda sitting at her desk, pouring a dark brew from her thermos flask. It was the one time in the day she would stop and talk, though she never revealed much about herself. How did I not know she had a daughter?

"And these are two of her paintings," Tom says, pointing to two country scenes that adorn the walls. "Such a very talented lady. And so generous too, always thinking of others."

I think of the prickly woman I knew, always nagging on at me to get out, to make friends, to get a life, and wonder whether I really knew her at all.

"So, have you got in touch with your parents yet?" Linda was on typical form.

I sighed. "What?"

"Come on. You've got a face like a wet weekend. I'm not daft you know. It's weeks since your mum called you." She took a long sip of coffee. "Well? Don't you want to speak to her?"

"How would you know what I want?"

Linda raised her eyebrows. "Seriously, Meg. What's the problem?"

I didn't answer.

"I mean, it's up to you," she said. "If you want to live your life like this-"

"Linda, please!"

"Fine!" She raised a hand to silence me. "Your choice. And maybe you're right. I mean, I don't know. Maybe she deserves it. Maybe. But do you deserve this?"

I frowned. "What do you mean?"

"OK, so your boyfriend left you-"

"Fiancé."

"Boyfriend, fiancé." She shrugged. "And now you've fallen out with your mum. Right?"

I didn't answer, but that didn't stop her.

"What I'm saying is this: you only have one life. It's up to you to choose how you live it. But don't let it pass you by just because you're too proud to make your peace with the past."

I turned back to my computer, my eyes burning. I could feel the weight of her gaze upon me as she sipped her coffee, but she said no more. Would I have let her go on, I wonder, if I'd known it was to be the last time I saw her?

It's a couple of hours before Ruth finally gets to me. "I'm sorry," she says, shutting the door behind a small group of guests. There are just a few of us left, mainly family as far as I can tell.

I shuffle uncomfortably and adjust the smile on my face.

"I'll go and dig it out now," she says. I glance at my watch, hoping it doesn't take too much digging.

To my relief, she's back in two minutes, a piece of paper in her hand.

"Here," she says, handing it to me.

I glance down at it and my breath catches in my throat. The pencil lines are bold and confident, but the subject is not. She is sad; her eyes gaze out of the page, revealing her vulnerability. I realise now how perceptive Linda really was. And I finally see myself through her eyes: lonely, stubborn, locked into a prison of my own making.

The tears well in my eyes, but it is not Linda I'm crying for but myself, for the years of pain and hurt, for the way I've been treated by others and the way I've treated myself.

"Thank you," I say, reaching out a hand, feeling the warmth of Ruth's skin against mine.

All Our Fragile Yesterdays

The man smiles when I open the door. His hand is raised to knock again, but he swiftly moves it to his hat, which he sweeps from his head.

"Mags! So lovely to see you!" he says, putting his suitcase down.

I peer at him, taking in his lively eyes, his broad nose, his neatly trimmed moustache. "Derek?" I say, slowly. Derek's the only one who ever called me Mags. But he doesn't look like Derek. And anyway, this can't be Derek. He's dead, as Judith tells me every time I forget.

Sometimes I wish she wouldn't tell me, that she'd let me think he'd just popped out for the newspaper. But she's wedded to the truth, that girl. She's off in search of it right now, chasing after a big story for her magazine. She left me a note to remind me, so I wouldn't worry when she didn't come home.

"You'll be ok, won't you?" she said anxiously before she got into her car and drove away. I had the impression she'd asked the same thing many times before, but I don't remember. I don't remember much these days. At least, not for long.

"I'm Jack," the man says, coughing into a neatly pressed handkerchief. He quickly folds it and puts it in his breast pocket, but not before I've seen the blood spots staining the pale material. He takes a deep breath and smiles. "Jack Allister. Derek and I were in the forces together."

"Of course you were!" I say, though I don't remember. But he has a kind face.

I open the door and let him in.

"You did what?" I can hear the panic in my voice and try to calm myself for Mum's sake. There's nothing I can do from 50 miles away. Except call the police. Should I call the police? "Tell me again," I say.

"His name's Jack. He stayed over last night. He was no bother at all. He's just gone out to visit Derek's grave. He asked if I wanted to go with him, but I said no."

So, he's out of the house. That's good.

"Did he say when he was coming back?" I say, trying to keep my voice light.

"Oh no. I suppose he'll be back when he gets hungry."

"Right." I chew my lip. Should I tell her to bolt the door? Would she even remember to do it? No, I decide. Better to act like nothing's wrong. "Your dinner's in the fridge, remember?" I say. "Four minutes in the microwave, and careful not to burn yourself."

"I'm not a child, Judith."

"No, Mum," I say. "Love you." Then I hang up the

phone and dash to my car.

"Derek?" I call when the sound of the key in the door wakes me from my nap. But of course it's not Derek. It can't be Derek.

"It's me. Judith." She sounds breathless. "Are you okay?" She leans over me and studies my face.

I pull her in for a kiss. "Fine, darling."

"No sign of Jack?"

"Jack?"

She sits down heavily beside me and takes my hand. "Your visitor. Dad's friend."

I shake my head, unsure what she means.

"Did he come back, Mum?" she says.

"Come back?"

"Yes, after visiting Dad's grave?"

I frown at her and shake my head. "I've been here on my own all day, darling."

She turns away then. She thinks I don't see her wipe the tear from her eye. But she doesn't need to cry for me. I'm not lonely. I have my memories to keep me company.

I walk around the house from room to room. Nothing seems to be out of place. Mum's wedding ring is still on the chain around her neck. There are few other valuables. Everything has been sold off, bit by bit, to pay for Mum's care. It'll be the house next. So, what on earth did he come for?

If he even exists, I remind myself. Perhaps he's just another figment of Mum's imagination, another figure conjured up from the past.

I leave the spare bedroom until last.

The curtains are closed when I open the door, but I can see that the bed has been slept in and there's a musky tang in the air. I move over to the window to throw open the curtains and that's when I see it: a small, blue suitcase perched upon the chair.

I exhale, my heart beating fast and kneel in front of it, my hands caressing the leather. Should I open it? It feels like an invasion of privacy, but surely I have nothing to apologise for on that count.

"Who are you, Jack?" I say out loud. "And why did you come here now?"

A few short minutes later, I have the answers to all my questions and a pain in my heart that will never completely fade. I wonder what he said to Mum last night, whether she understood on any level who this man was, how his act of contrition towards my father constituted in its own way a further betrayal.

I put the letter down and stare at the contents of the suitcase, knowing they could change our lives and yet... And yet, I can't accept this. We can't accept this. Not from him. Not even knowing that we will never see him again, that he'll never know my decision.

I put the letter back in the suitcase and close the lid.

"Are you going somewhere, dear?" I say when I see Judith come down the stairs, a suitcase in her hand. I frown. I feel sure I've seen that suitcase before.

"No, Mum," she says, not meeting my eye.

"Oh." I raise an eyebrow at her. "You've just come back," I say.

"Yes, Mum," she says, walking out into the garden.

There's a cold wind blowing so I'm surprised when I see her light the barbecue. I'm even more surprised when she opens the case and tips its contents onto the flames. Pieces of paper fly into the air; some look like bank notes. I let out a gasp, but then I realise my mistake. It must be Monopoly money. She and Derek used to love playing Monopoly.

The wind whips at the papers, scattering them across the lawn. A photograph flies free and is plastered against the window. In it, two men in uniform stand side by side, smiling at the camera. They look happy together, their spines straight, their fingertips almost touching. The man on the right has a kind face, but it's the man on the left I can't tear my eyes away from.

The wind drops, and with it the photograph.

I sigh and turn back to the television.

Julia Graves

Grey

Everything's grey. The sky, covered in clouds, is grey. The road, slick with morning rain, is grey. But most of all, my mind is grey.

It's got so bad that I almost expect, when I look in the mirror, for my skin to be grey and my hair too. It's almost a surprise to glance up and see the rosy glow of my cheeks and the chestnut curls that still bounce around them. To look at me, you wouldn't think anything was wrong. But inside, there is only grey.

It's not so bad when the car's moving. The traffic rolls along and my mind rolls along with it, my eyes on the road ahead, my thoughts on what I'm doing: each gear shift, each nudge of the accelerator, each tap on the brakes. But then we come to a standstill and the red of the brake lights ahead penetrates the grey and it's like an assault on the senses. It's more than I can bear. I want to rip my skin off and escape, run away from the car, away from my body, away from myself, but I can't. All I can do is sit here and wait and try to maintain my sanity, if I've any left to maintain.

You're probably waiting for some great revelation, that my husband has left me or my baby's got a rare disease or my dog's died and I'm in crisis, but no. The truth is that nothing has happened. I still have a job. I still have a flat to live in, a husband who loves me (although never quite enough) and a best friend I can call any time, night or day. So why do I feel like this?

Don't worry, you're not alone. I've heard it all before. "Your life's fine, Shannon," they say, or, "Think of the starving children in Africa." And I know.

I know.

It's true. My life's fine. Not brilliant, but fine. And that's what makes it all the worse. Worse because there's no one thing I can focus on, nothing I can 'fix' to make it all okay again. Worse because I can feel the judgement being passed upon me. Worse because I judge myself.

And then I laugh at something they say in the office and you can almost hear the sighs of relief. Great, they think. She's okay now. But I'm not. The greyness comes and goes like a mist, sometimes thick, sometimes thin, but it's always there and it can swallow me up without warning.

I remember when I was little and Louise Silverton's mum was found dead of an overdose, a note clutched in her hand. None of us knew what to say to Louise when she came back to school, or whether to say anything at all. The teachers tried to prepare us, but I don't think they knew what to say either.

I know now that Louise's mother didn't want to go. She didn't take her own life. The greyness took it from her, draining it of colour until there was nothing left but grey.

I wondered at first how Louise managed to carry on, why she was always the first to arrive at every party and the last to leave, unless she met a young man, of course, as she often did. Then baby number one was joined by baby number two and still she was going out partying, and I frowned at her recklessness, her lack of responsibility. I can see now that she was trying to fight back against the grey before it could get hold of her too.

For me, there is no such fight. For me, it is all I can do to keep my car pointing in the right direction and drive, on and on, following the stream of tail lights that flicker and glow and burn my eyes, and I know they must keep burning because if they do not, there will be nothing left for me.

Only grey.

Julia Graves

Payback

"Here we go again!"

Vanessa flinches as Dave slams his hand down on the table, hard.

"You just have to be right, don't you? Every damn time!"

"Me?" Vanessa's voice is sharp, her reaction instinctive. Her eyes glint dangerously, but Dave continues to stare back at her, a challenge on his face.

Vanessa laughs bitterly, a laugh that could shred steel. "Perhaps you should take a look in the mirror some time."

She swallows as soon as the words have left her mouth, the fear rising in her as Dave calmly studies her face, a look of hatred in his eyes.

"Now you're just being childish," he says coldly.

Vanessa tries to hold his gaze, but her eyes slip away, back to the surface of the table, as they start to fill with tears. She rubs furiously at them with the back of her hand.

Dave snorts. "Go on, turn the waterworks on. I've seen it all before. It won't wash with me any more. I'm past caring."

"Get out then!"

Vanessa springs to her feet like a tiger released from its cage. She feels her frayed nerves snap and suddenly, she is no longer afraid.

"Go on! Go!" she shouts, her voice full of rage. "Call yourself a husband?"

She shakes her head. "You're no kind of a husband! You don't care about anyone but yourself. And to think I've stuck with you for all these years."

Dave's voice, when he speaks again, is quiet, but none the less menacing for it.

"You've stuck with me?" He laughs. "What about me?" he says. "I'm sick of trying to pick you up all the time, sick of trying to keep you happy. Do you have any idea what a burden you've become? And then you're surprised I want a bit of fun?"

It's been an open secret that Dave has had affairs over the years. Vanessa has hardened herself to the knowledge. In some ways, she almost welcomed it: after all, if he was getting his kicks elsewhere, perhaps he wouldn't feel the need to force himself on her late at night, in the dark. But this is the first time he has admitted it to her face, and Vanessa feels it like a hammer blow, driving home the final nail in the coffin of her marriage.

No longer can she pretend there is any love or respect of any kind between them. She has become everything she despised in her own mother and the realisation defeats her.

Vanessa's face crumples as she sinks back into her chair. The tears are no longer a trickle but a flood.

She holds her face in her hands and sobs, barely flinching when the door slams, not moving when she hears the car door bang or the roar of the engine.

But when he has finally gone and there is nothing but silence, she takes the knife from the drawer and carries it into the bedroom.

Vanessa's eyes flicker when the bedroom door creaks open and her breathing quickens but she doesn't move. She lies, rigid, as Dave makes his way round to his side of the bed, cursing as he trips over a slipper carelessly discarded by her nightstand.

She listens to him peeling off his clothes and throwing them on the floor.

She feels the mattress dip as he sits heavily on the edge of the bed before sliding himself under the covers.

She holds her breath as he grunts in the darkness, dreading the touch of his clammy hand on her skin. Even when it doesn't come there is no relief, no certainty that she won't wake in the night to find him pressing himself into her.

As he begins to snore, Vanessa exhales, long and hard. She wonders how he can just come back and carry on each time, how he can continue to act like nothing has changed.

"Not this time," she whispers into the darkness, still clutching the knife in her hand. "Not this time."

Three hours later she is in a brightly lit cafe, a suitcase by her side, her handbag balanced on her knee. At the next table, children squabble over the last pancake, but Vanessa barely notices.

She stirs at her coffee for long minutes, her eyes glazed, staring into space, before finally putting the spoon down and taking a sip. She grimaces at the taste but swigs the rest back all the same.

Placing the cup down on her tray, she shudders.

"Are you all right, love?" The waitress is looking at Vanessa kindly, her head tipped to one side.

"I'm fine," Vanessa says, not meeting her eye. She glances down at her hand, at the pale band of skin where her wedding ring used to be. She clasps her hands together to stop them shaking.

The waitress's lips part as if she's about to ask another question, but instead she nods, smiles and moves on to clean the next table.

The tannoy announcement rings out through the speakers in the corner of the cafe. "Flight BA247 to Sao Paulo now boarding at gate 3."

Vanessa glances around but there is no sign of trouble. Relieved, she picks up her bags and heads for the gate.

Teddy Bear

I knew as soon as I saw the teddy bear that I had to have it, or rather, the baby had to have it. I didn't yet know whether I was expecting a boy or a girl. It didn't matter. I just knew he - or she - would love the bear either way.

It was small, blue and brown, with raggedy ears and a button nose. It was a strange-looking thing, but cute, nonetheless. It would fit right into our family.

I put it on the dashboard of my car as I drove home and talked to it as if it were my child. He didn't reply, just looked at me with that funny look on his face. I loved him.

At home, I headed straight to the nursery and placed him on top of the toy box.

Only a few days earlier this had been my home office. Now the filing cabinet and desk had gone, the dull blue walls had been painted lilac and adorned with nursery-rhyme character transfers. I threw open the curtains to let in the light and nodded with satisfaction. Then I left, not quite closing the door behind me.

Petra was a big bear of a dog we'd adopted two years earlier. She wouldn't hurt a fly, I told parents regularly when she approached the children at the playground, her big, wet tongue hanging out, her tail wagging energetically. And it was true.

It wasn't her fault. She didn't set out to harm the bear. She was just curious.

She'd been used to sleeping under my desk during the day and hadn't been allowed into the newly decorated room for fear of her hair contaminating the paintwork. But now, as she snuffled around, she found the door open. It was only natural that she should wander in.

I realised my mistake straight away, as soon as I heard the door creak open. I rushed to grab her, but it was too late. She was already inside, eyes fixed on the bear, muzzle open to scoop him up.

Not stopping to think, I launched myself across the room.

It's strange, waking up in hospital.

At first, you don't quite know where you are. Then, when your eyes finally manage to focus on the familiar face leaning over you, on his red-rimmed eyes and the gloomy set of his mouth, you realise where you are. Slowly, horrifyingly, you remember why you are there.

Worst of all, when you see him close his eyes, see that tiny shake of his head, you know what you have done. And your whole world collapses in on itself.

It was hard coming home, hard to see my sorrow reflected back at me in Petra's big eyes.

It is still hard being here, confronted daily by the sight of the nursery door.

One day, I will go in there again.

One day, I will hold a child in my arms and smile as I give him his very first teddy bear.

One day.

Julia Graves

Stronger

It's a Thursday when it happens. I won't say a Thursday like any other, as there hasn't been such a thing as an ordinary Thursday - or any ordinary day - since the accident. There have been good days and bad days, days when the pain has been intense and days when it has lessened, not in a linear way like you might imagine, but ebbing and flowing like a river.

This is a bad pain day, so when I hear the doorbell ring, I ignore it. But when the key scrapes in the lock, I smile. It must be Rosie.

Rosie, my friend and neighbour, has been my rock ever since the accident. I wait to hear her familiar call of, "Yoo hoo, I'll put the kettle on, shall I?" but it doesn't come. Instead I hear the heavy tread of footsteps on the stairs and I shrink back, my heart pounding. Then I hear John's voice calling me, and it's an echo from the past.

I shake my head. I must be imagining it. But then I turn to look and there he is, framed in the doorway to my bedroom - *our* bedroom - and it feels so familiar and yet so very wrong.

The accident came out of nowhere. It was a grey and frosty morning; I was driving alone when a car ploughed into the side of mine. I don't remember the impact. I don't remember much about the journey at all. But even now I experience a sense of panic whenever I pass that junction, the horror of the moment coded into some primitive part of my brain.

Everything hurt when I woke up. Everything above the waist, that is. My arms, my back, even my lungs. But worse, much worse, was the fact that I couldn't feel my legs at all.

I tried to move but my body refused to obey. Even my head felt like stone, weighted down onto the pillow. A machine was beeping to my left, keeping a steady rhythm. I started to tremble. My right eye was swollen closed, the vision in my left blurry through the tears that welled and refused to fall.

"John?" I said. "John?" My voice was little more than a croak, but still, I expected some reply, to feel his hand on mine, to see his face appear in the space above mine. But none of that came.

"John?" I said again, but still he didn't answer.

I lay alone, counting to 100, over and over, waiting for him to appear until finally, exhausted, I drifted off into sleep.

When I awoke, a nurse was bustling around me, her pencil scratching against a clipboard.

"Oh!" she said when her eyes met mine. "Welcome back."

"My husband?" I said, my voice catching in my throat.

"Shh, shh," she said.

"Is he...?"

"Your husband?" She busied herself checking the tubes and lines that connected me to the machine. "I'm not sure where he is." She patted me on the arm, sending a shock of pain up through my shoulder. "You just rest."

"Not sure?"

She didn't reply.

Even then, I couldn't have imagined that he wouldn't be coming at all.

It was Rosie who told me he'd gone. "I'm sorry," she said. We both knew it wasn't enough.

I cried then, great sobs and gulps that racked me with physical pain to match the anguish of his abandonment.

I half expected that when I got home, there would be a note, a letter, something to explain his disappearance. If there was, I never found it.

As time went on, I came to accept that I might never hear from him again, and I never did. Until now.

"Hello Louise."

Hello? Is that the best he can manage?

I stare at him coldly. His dark hair is flecked with grey. His eyes look tired, his skin pale. I wonder where he's been for the past six months. I want him to hold me. I want him to kiss me. I want to pound my fists against his chest. I want to make him feel the pain I've had to live with since he left.

"What are you doing here?" I say.

He frowns. "You're looking..."

I cross my arms and tip my head on one side, glancing over at my walking frame. I wince as a spike of pain shoots up my spine, but John doesn't seem to notice. He studies his feet, shifting his weight from one to the other.

"I'm..." He shakes his head. "I didn't mean..."

"You didn't mean to walk out when I needed you most?"

His head shoots up, the hurt clear in his eyes. "That's not-"

"Fair?" I challenge him.

He sighs. "I'm sorry Lou. I didn't know what to do."

"So, you thought the best option was to leave?"

He shrugs, leaning against the doorframe, twiddling his wedding ring between finger and thumb. I glance at my bare ring finger, wondering whether he's noticed, but when I look back up, he's staring at the ceiling. He sighs. "I couldn't cope, seeing you like that."

"*You* couldn't cope?"

Again, he shakes his head. "I'm sorry," he says finally. He takes a deep breath and I try to read his expression, but he looks as bewildered as I feel. "Can we...?"

"Can we what?"

"I love you, Lou."

He loves me.

He left me.

He's back.

But why is he back? Why is he doing this to me? Do I even know him any more? Can I ever trust him again?

I put a hand on my forehead and hug the other arm around me.

"I can't do this," I say. "I think you should go."

It's only later that I allow myself to cry. The tears come in waves, hot, furious tears at first, followed by calmer, sorrowful ones. But I know that I did what I had to do.

"And he just walked right into your bedroom?"

"Pretty much."

"Wow." Rosie puffs out her cheeks. "Well, good for you," she says, "sending him packing."

I let out a bitter laugh I barely recognise as my own.

"So, what now?" she says.

"Now I carry on."

She nods and I smile to myself. At least she seems to accept that as a possibility. I know what she thinks. I've learnt to walk again. Learning to live without John should be the easy part. But she's wrong.

"Do you think you've seen the last of him?"

I shrug. "It depends what story he's telling himself," I say. "But yeah, I think so." I pick a piece of lint from my jeans, anything to avoid meeting her eye. "He can tell himself he tried. It was my decision to send him away. That's got to be enough to soothe his conscience."

"You think that's all it was?"

"I don't know. I guess."

"Well, good riddance," she says. "You're better off without him."

I smile and nod, my face a mask.

He's gone. And now there is nothing for it but to wait and see. I've coped without him so far. Hard as it seems, I know the days will come and go, and if I have to face them alone, that's just what I will do.

And if he does come back? I suppress the thought. If I've learnt anything over the last six months, it is to take things one step at a time.

I am stronger now than I have ever been.

George's Case

The last time I saw George, he was five. I'd put him in his favourite shorts and t-shirt for his best friend's party and washed and brushed his blond hair, feeling him wriggle in my lap as I pulled the brush through the curls forming around his neck.

"Time you had a haircut, Mister," I said, reaching for my scissors but he squirmed away from me, tugging at my hand and giggling excitedly as we made our way outside to the car.

"Behave yourself," I said as we pulled up outside Freddie's house. "And have fun." I leaned across to plant a kiss on his head, but already he'd gone, slamming the car door behind him and scurrying up the path to knock on the front door.

"See you later," I called out of the car window, waving to Freddie's mum as George slipped through the crack in the door and disappeared into the house, not stopping to take off his sandals.

It was when I got home I realised he'd forgotten to take Freddie's present. A thousand times I've asked myself whether it would have made a difference if he'd remembered it, if I'd reminded him, if I'd gone back with it straight away instead of putting it next to the door to take later.

I'm sure Freddie's mum must have realised it was a mistake; I can't believe she would have let the other kids pick on him. But why else, I asked myself, would a five year-old boy leave a party he'd been looking forward to for weeks and start walking?

He never made it home.

When George's case was opened, it was as a missing person. We all knew it was more than that. We knew because he'd never run away before. We knew because he was a happy little boy who was right where he wanted to be. But there was always just enough room for doubt, because of that forgotten present. Although the other children denied it, I couldn't shake the feeling that words had been exchanged.

I sat on the stairs for the rest of the afternoon, waiting, hoping for George to come wandering up the street. But when the knock on the door did come, it was a small, dark-eyed police officer, who made me tea and told me not to worry, that lots of children run away.

"Not George," I told her.

When George's father came home, later than usual and several pints the worse for wear, he looked shocked to see the police car outside and almost angry to see the police woman inside, sitting with me as I knitted George's jumper, taking comfort from the familiar click-click of the needles and the feel of the wool on my skin.

"What is it, Pauline?" he said, his large frame filling the doorway, his features pulled into a frown. "What's he done?"

"What's who done?"

The policewoman was quickly on her feet. "WPC Denise Mitchell," she said, holding out her hand.

Derek looked at it disdainfully before turning back to me again.

"What's who done?" I repeated.

He looked from me to Denise and back again. "Well?" he demanded. "It's George, isn't it?"

It was only then I realised he didn't know. "Yes," I said, swollen eyes filling, once again, with tears.

"I knew it. What's he gone and done now?"

"He's..." I swallowed, hard, feeling the panic start to build.

"Sit down, Mr Stewart," Denise suggested, gently.

"I don't want to sit down," Derek said. "George!" he called, leaning out into the hallway to shout up the stairs. "George! Get down here right now!"

"He's..." I gulped. "He's not there."

"Not there?"

"Mr Stewart," Denise said, more firmly now. "George has gone missing."

"Missing?" Derek glared at her, as if she were speaking a foreign language.

"He's probably just run away or got lost..."

"Probably?"

Denise flapped her arms but said nothing.

"Not George," I said, tears erupting again. "Not

George."

At first, suspicion fell on a delivery driver who had been seen loitering in the street that morning. Perhaps he'd followed us to Freddie's house, Denise suggested gently.

No, I said. Nobody had followed us.

But could I be sure?

Derek got changed as soon as he heard the news and headed out to join the hunt. But nothing was found that day, or the next. The delivery driver was questioned and released. No evidence could be found against him. No evidence, it seemed, could be found at all. It was as if George had simply vanished into thin air.

I prayed for there to be a breakthrough, for some hint of what might have happened to my little Georgie. I lay in bed at night, listening to Derek snore and asking myself those same questions over and over again. Could I have prevented this? What if I'd taken the present round? What if...?

But it was no good. No answers were forthcoming. Nothing changed; nothing could change until some small piece of evidence was found. Time seemed to have been suspended; collectively we held our breath. I prayed for a breakthrough that would move the case forward.

But then his sandals were found and there was no going back.

Kidnap. Murder. Such harsh words. Such cruel words. They had been there all along, of course, unspoken beneath the pleasantries and the questions and the accusing looks.

But who would want to harm my Georgie?

"Who said anything about murder?" Derek snapped at me over his bowl of breakfast cereal. "He probably just wandered off and got lost."

"For three days?" I wailed. "And what about his sandals?"

"Hmm." Derek grunted. "But it's only a pair of shoes. And there wasn't any blood. No need to panic."

"No need to panic?" I could hear the hysteria rising in my voice. "What, so you think Georgie just got a bit hot and decided to kick his shoes off?"

"Don't be sarcastic, Pauline, it doesn't suit you."

I sat, head in hands, wondering when George would be found, praying that despite the odds he would be found alive and well. Every crunch of Derek's teeth on his cereal grated on my nerves.

"Shouldn't you be getting back out there?" I said eventually.

"Hmm?"

"Won't they have started searching again by now?"

He shrugged, flicking through the pages of his newspaper. "Probably."

"So?"

He looked up at me, spoon dangling from his hand, splashing drops of milk onto the newspaper. "What's the point?" he said.

"What?"

Derek slammed his newspaper closed. "OK, OK, you win." And with that he shoved his chair back, its wooden legs screeching against the tiled floor, and strode out the door, leaving me to stare at the picture of George on the front page.

Tears leaked from my eyes as I fought the suspicion that he was glad George was gone, realising painfully that I was alone in my grief for a child who might yet be alive.

If I thought back then that finding George's body was the worst thing that could have happened, I was wrong. Not finding him was far worse.

Derek and I didn't have a big bust up. He just started coming home later and later at night, until he didn't come home at all.

"It's not uncommon for the parents of missing children to experience some marital difficulties," Denise told me. I was grateful for the use of the word 'missing' but we both knew that the damage to the marriage was terminal.

The doctor prescribed me sleeping pills and a programme of counselling. Somehow, slowly, I dragged myself out of the pit of despair and when I found out that Derek had moved in with a girl from the Stilwell Estate, I was frankly relieved. But George's loss wasn't so easy to come to terms with.

Weeks turned into months and months into years and still there was no news. The press quickly lost interest and the public too. Even the police stopped asking questions. I was alone with my memories and my fading hopes.

Slowly, slowly, my memories of George dimmed until I could no longer remember the smell of his hair or the feel of his skin. And I knew that if, by some miracle, he was returned to me, he would no longer be the small boy I had held in my arms. But that didn't stop me praying he would come back.

It was twenty years after George's disappearance that the knock on the door came. I opened it with one hand, a pan of beans in the other. When I saw him standing there, I almost lost my grip. I set the pan down on the telephone shelf, sending a cascade of leaflets floating to the floor.

He bent to pick them up and handed them back to me, smiling shyly.

"Mrs Stewart?" he said.

"Yes," I said, my eyes not leaving his face. I knew, of course, that he was not George, but the likeness was remarkable: the shape of his eyes, the gentle curve of his shy smile, the colour of his hair. Ironic, that George should have looked so much like the father who never wanted him.

"I'm Stephen. Stephen –"

"Stewart." I said softly. "Of course. Come in."

I led him to the kitchen where he glanced at the pan of sausages frying on the hob. "It's not a bad time, is it?"

"No," I said, flicking off the gas and signalling for him to take a seat at the kitchen table. "Drink?" I offered, reluctant to take my seat opposite him.

"No. Thank you." He paused. "I suppose you're wondering why I'm here."

"I suppose I am," I said quietly, though what other reason could there be but George?

"You probably know that my father died last week."

I nodded. You don't live in the same town as your ex-husband without hearing things, however much you might not want to. When he has children, for example. When he's diagnosed with cancer. When he dies in an alcohol-fuelled accident. But you don't expect one of his children to turn up on your doorstep.

"Were you close?" I said, barely at a whisper.

He stared at me for a moment before shaking his head. "No," he said, and I felt the relief coursing through my veins. Why should it matter to me? I wondered. It didn't bring George back.

"Did he tell you?" I said. "About..."

"George," he said softly, and I was touched to see the concern that clouded his face. "He told us at the end. My sister, Lucy and me."

I sat and digested that information, wondering why he had not told them before; why he chose to tell them at all. For long moments the only sound was the ticking of the clock, but I knew there was more.

"I can go," Stephen said, finally. "Or I can come back another time."

"No," I said. "Tell me."

He took a deep breath, steeling himself, perhaps, to impart news that could be painful to me, but there was no new pain to be suffered.

"It was him, wasn't it?" I said. It was a thought I had suppressed many times before, but suddenly I knew it to be true. What else could have brought Stephen to me? "He killed my George."

"Yes." Tears rolled down his nose and splashed onto the surface of the table. "He said it was an accident but-"

I glanced up, frowning and he stopped himself.

"I'm so sorry," he said.

I allowed my thoughts to drift back through the years. Should I have seen it coming? I wondered. Could I have done anything - *anything?* - to prevent it? And all the time the police were asking their questions... How could I not have known?

"You can't think like that," Stephen said, and it was only then I realised I had spoken aloud. "It's not your fault," he insisted. "He's the one to blame."

"Did he... hurt you?"

Stephen shook his head slowly, then shrugged. "He hit us. He drank. He was mentally abusive, I guess. But we're the lucky ones."

I bowed my head, taking his hand in mine, noticing the smoothness of his skin. He didn't pull away. "I'm sorry," I said.

What more did he know? I wondered. Had Derek revealed where George was buried? How he had died? Why his shoes had been found? I opened my mouth to speak but only a long groan came out. Would it help to know? I wondered.

"What... will you do?" Stephen said, his voice shaking.
"Do?"
"Will you tell the police?"
"Huh?"
He sighed, shuffling in his seat. "Dad's accident..." he said and suddenly I understood.
"Was an accident," I said, squeezing his hand. "No more police. No more questions. It's over."
"Thank you," he whispered, leaning in to give me a final hug before scurrying down the hallway and out of my life.
I watched him leave, that boy who could have been my son. I watched him leave and I smiled through the tears.
Maybe, one day, George's case will be closed. In time.

No Rescue

Amy sat and listened to the waves breaking on the shore. The sun had long since sunk behind the cliffs, gone for another day. Even the seabirds had settled down to sleep. Only Amy remained, sitting, listening, counting the waves as they sucked at the shingle, drawing it back, then spitting it out again.

A cold wind blew, and she pulled her coat around her. She wondered how long it would take for Colin to join her, to sit and rest his head on her shoulder, just as he had done a thousand times before.

"You bitch!"

She could still hear the anger in his voice as he had loosed his parting shot, making her tremble though the words had long since lost their power. She could still hear the slam of the door and feel the hardness of the wood as she had crumpled against it, exhausted but strangely elated.

It still hurt when he snapped and yet it was endlessly fascinating to see just how far she could push him. And tonight, she had pushed him hard.

"Amy." His voice was soft as he clambered down the rocks towards her. Her breath quickened as he approached, yet her eyes stayed fixed on the moonbeams bouncing off the water. "Amy."

He stood next to her, shuffling from foot to foot and she felt her irritation rise again. This wasn't how it was supposed to be.

"Amy," he said again, his voice more urgent now, and finally she was forced to tear her gaze away from the water and onto his face, his beautiful, tear-streaked face. Still he didn't sit; still he didn't bend.

She frowned and tilted her head to get a better look at him, trying to understand what was different this time.

"I'm sorry."

Different, and yet the same. The flame of triumph flickered inside her and she smiled, patting the rock beside her, but he shook his head.

"I'm sorry," he said again, holding out his hand.

Instinctively, she reached out to him, but his warm flesh slipped away, leaving only the coldness of metal. Then he turned and walked away, leaving her to stare, dumbstruck, at the key in her hand. She turned it over and over, running her thumb along its bumps and ridges, letting them dig into her skin, the physical pain distracting her from the emptiness inside. Her stomach heaved and rolled with the sea and she closed her eyes, breathing in the salty air.

The moon crept out from behind a cloud, spotlighting her as effectively as the beam of a lighthouse, but there was no rescue. She had toyed with the rocks for too long and now she was lost.

She sat, gaze fixed ahead, as the waves crashed onto the shore.

The Dinner Party

Jane stepped back and admired herself in the mirror. She ran a hand through her hair and smiled. Though still short, it was full of body and framed her face beautifully. She had been devastated to lose her long blond curls, but she was starting to get used to this new look, just as she was starting to get used to her new life.

She pulled her shawl around her shoulders and smiled with satisfaction at how perfectly it matched her new dress. Sandy had said there was no need to dress up, but for Jane, this was quite an event, and she wanted to look her best for it.

"Now then," she said to herself, taking a deep breath and nodding at her reflection. "You can do this."

The taxi driver was chatty, but Jane's short replies seemed to give him the message that she didn't want to talk and soon he lapsed into silence. She looked out of the window, watching the city's streets slide by. It was bigger than her hometown, with more shops, more bright lights, more people. More opportunities to be anonymous, she had thought, but still a part of her wished she had ended up somewhere smaller, where she didn't have to keep looking over her shoulder all the time.

It had taken several months for her to feel at home here, for the nightmares to stop, for her to start trusting people again. At first, she had been convinced that he would find her, that one day she would turn around and see his stooped frame following her up the street, or spy his thin fingers on her window ledge, his sharp green eyes peering in. But gradually she had overcome her fears, and when Sandy had joined the company, a bond had formed between them, the two newest members of the team.

The car slowed to a halt and she peered out at the row of Victorian terraced houses, trying to guess which might be Sandy's.

"Number seventeen." The taxi driver nodded towards an imposing mid-terrace house with smart new windows and a BMW parked outside. "Have a good evening," he said as she climbed out of the car and smoothed down her dress. She waited until he'd driven away before opening the garden gate and clipping her way up the path.

"Jane!" The door was flung open before she even reached it and Sandy gave her a big hug, then ushered her through to the living room.

"Hello." Sandy's husband, Dylan, was chatting on the sofa with a guy Jane recognised from the office and a lady with a long red ponytail and even redder lipstick, who was introduced as his wife.

Jane smiled hello and settled into the armchair in the corner, accepting a glass of wine and helping herself to a handful of nuts from the elegant glass bowl on the table.

"Your house is beautiful, Sandy," she said, looking round at the matching curtains and cushions and the tasteful paintings on the wall.

Sandy beamed. "Of course, you've not been here before! Here, let me show you round."

The rest of the house was every bit as impressive as the living room, from the stunning granite worktop in the kitchen to the beautiful, handmade wardrobes in the master bedroom. "And you crocheted this blanket yourself?" Jane asked incredulously, running a hand over the soft woollen blanket on the spare bed in the attic room.

"Yes." She could hear the pride in her friend's voice. "It's easy. I'll show you some time."

"I'd like that." Jane smiled easily, feeling relaxed in Sandy's company.

"Great. Now listen," Sandy plopped herself down on the bed and signalled for Jane to sit down beside her. "I know you wanted us to keep this evening small - and we have," she added quickly, "but Dylan has invited one more person. He's new at work and Dylan felt sorry for him."

"Oh," Jane swallowed. "Okay. As long as it's not meant to be a set-up."

"Set-up?" Sandy asked, a twinkle in her eye.

"Oh, you!" Jane tried to smile but she could feel the tension in her stomach. "What's his name?" she asked, her voice emerging as little more than a squeak.

"It's John," Sandy said, frowning. "Are you okay, Jane? You look ever so pale."

"I'm fine." And as she headed down the stairs, she tried to tell herself that she was, but when she heard the doorbell and the sound of male voices, she had to steady herself against the wall and catch her breath. But his accent was Scottish, not the Midlands twang that haunted her nightmares, and when she emerged into the living room, there he was: tall, with dark hair and twinkling eyes. Just the sort of man she'd be interested in if she were looking for a relationship.

The evening passed companionably and when her taxi pulled up outside and she stepped out into the cool night air, she had to admit she had enjoyed it.

"We'll have to do it again some time," Sandy said, and Jane smiled her agreement.

As she settled into the back seat of the taxi, it was John's face that floated in front of her eyes, John's voice that echoed in her ears. She couldn't help laughing at the memory of his off-the-wall impressions, his wacky sense of humour. And he'd asked if he could call her! Maybe her luck was changing at last.

The taxi pulled off slowly at first, gaining speed and it was only when it turned left instead of right that she realised she hadn't given her address.

"Oh, sorry," she said with a yawn, suddenly exhausted. "You've gone the wrong way."

"No, Jane." The familiar Midlands voice was calm, quiet, chilling. "I know exactly where we're going."

The Last Exhibition

"Look!" Colin says, pressing his nose up to the painting. "Just look at those brush strokes!" He takes a step back. "And his use of light and shade is incredible. Just amazing."

"Yes," I say, smiling. I'm no expert but his enthusiasm is infectious. "Isn't it?"

"What an achievement," he says, gesturing around at the paintings on the walls.

He sighs, the corners of his mouth drooping, and I can tell that he's comparing these masterpieces to his own works, knocked up in the garage between shifts in the warehouse. It's not a fair comparison, I want to tell him. Some artists dedicate their whole lives to their bodies of work. But with that thought comes the guilt that Roger and I couldn't afford to send him to art school, couldn't afford for him to do the same.

The painting in front of us is of a sunset, shades of pink and purple merging with the blue. It's no wonder Colin is drawn to it. It reminds me of the sketches he used to make night after night, never coming in for his dinner until the last rays had disappeared. He was such a good boy, never complaining, ever thoughtful. He used to bring me flowers, just like his father before him.

"You never told me he was so talented," Colin says, and I want to ask what he means, who he means, but the pain stabs my chest unmercifully. Perhaps it's just the guilt. Whatever it is, it takes my breath away.

"You go on," I say, trying to fix a smile on my face, knowing I won't be able to maintain it for long. "I'm just going to sit here a while."

"I should stay," he says, an anxious look on his face.

"No," I say before he has the chance to sit down beside me. It comes out more harshly than I intended. I take a deep breath.

"No," I say again, more gently, "you go on. Please." My cheeks ache with the effort of smiling; my eyes are beginning to fill with tears. I suppress the words 'I'm fine,' knowing they would be a red flag. He was so excited about bringing me to the library today. I don't remember why. He hasn't even picked out any books. But I refuse to spoil his day.

"Well, okay," he says, his hair swinging across in front of his eyes. I wish he would get a haircut. I barely recognise him lately. "Just this once won't hurt, I guess." He winks at me. "But don't tell the boss, eh?"

I open my mouth to ask what he's talking about, but the pain is too much. I nod and watch as he walks away, struggling to keep my body erect until he is out of sight and I can slump across the bench, breathing into the pain, gritting my teeth as another invisible wave passes through my body.

"Are you okay?" The man is short, well dressed. He is wearing a hat. Roger always wore a hat, though he used to have better style. I shall have to buy him a new one.

"Yes, yes," I say, trying to straighten up, not wanting Roger to see me like this. But it's no good. The pain has gripped my whole body.

I reach out a hand to take his, but he pulls away. "Roger?" I say. "Roger?" but he looks frightened and that scares me more than anything. Roger was always so brave, right up until he left. I can't think where he went now.

"Roger?" I say again, but he turns away, calling out loudly and there's a woman coming towards me now, a badge swinging around her neck.

"Mrs Fairweather?" she says. "Are you all right?" I know her face but I can't place her. Who is she and what's she doing with my Roger?

The colours are swirling in front of my eyes. I feel like I have been transported inside one of the paintings. The pain is starting to ease. My head feels light. I feel there is something I need to say before I drift away.

"My son's a painter," I tell the woman, grasping onto her hand urgently. "Such a bright boy, my Colin."

"Colin?" I hear her say through the fog of colours that swirl before my eyes. "Colin Fairweather?"

I nod and close my eyes, embracing the darkness.

I hear someone gasp. "The artist? But didn't he-?"

"Poor love," the woman's voice says. "Such a tragedy."

I'm floating now. I can feel their arms pulling me up, up, hear their voices calling to me in shades of lilac and pink.

"Colin," I say.

"I'm here, Mum."

Of course he's here. He was always here. I press a hand to my chest. Or is it someone else's hand? It's hard to tell now.

"Hold on," I say. "I won't be long."

Patient 52

He has his eyes closed when I approach the bed but somehow, I know he's awake. Perhaps he saw me coming. Perhaps he's trying to sleep. It doesn't matter. I have time to wait.

I study his face, or what I can see of it. A bandage covers the right side of his head. His eye peeks out from underneath, but it's bruised and swollen, the purple just starting to fade to yellow around the edges. His face is lined with wrinkles, his skin spotted with age.

I glance up at the name above the bed: Ronald Taylor. I'm in the right place.

"Well?" His gruff voice takes me by surprise. I look up to see one piercing blue eye staring right at me. The other remains closed. "Have you come to flog me TV credits?"

"Um, no," I say, smoothing down my skirt.

"Huh. One of them bible bashers then."

"No," I laugh. "Not one of them either. I'm Julie," I say, holding out my hand. "I'm a visitor."

"Ron," he says, taking my hand in his and shaking it with a surprisingly firm grip. He glances round the ward. "Who's yours then?"

"None of them," I say, smiling. "I'm here to visit you."

"Me?" He looks puzzled.

I laugh. "Heard you hadn't seen anyone but the nurses for a couple of days and thought you might fancy a fresh face."

He nods. "Well," he says slowly. "Lucky me."

It's 4am when I wake from the dream. In it, we walk hand in hand through the zoo, my father and me. I chatter away and he tries to keep smiling but I can feel the sadness coming off him in waves.

"What's wrong, Dad?" I ask when we sit down in the cafe, him with a black coffee, me with the large ice cream I've always hankered after.

He shakes his head and smiles but the sadness lurks in his eyes.

"Daddy?" I say, the worry pressing down on my chest.

He takes a deep breath and runs a hand through his hair. "Look, sweetheart," he says. "You know that Mummy and I haven't been getting on lately."

I know they've argued. I've heard them hissing at each other in the kitchen late at night. But what's new? It's always like this when his black moods come, and Mummy's seemed so much brighter this time.

I shrug and he sighs. "Look, there isn't an easy way of saying this," he says. I can see his lips move and I know what they must be saying - that he's going to New Zealand; that I have to stay with Mummy; that I can visit him in the summer - but all I can hear is the rush of blood in my ears and I know that things will never, ever be the same again.

It's two days before I visit Ron again. His bandage has been removed and though the bruising is starting to fade, he still looks bashed up and exhausted.

"Good of you to come back," he says, smiling.

"It's what I do."

We sit and chat. He tells me about his son, about his dog. The dog died. The son moved away. He lives on his own now.

I tell him my dad died when I was young. I spare him the details. "Then the cancer took my mum," I say. "Now I'm alone too."

"A pretty thing like you," he says.

I shrug. "It's not so bad. I have friends. I meet people. I'm not lonely."

"Lucky you." He scratches his neck and I can see he's chewing something over. "I'd like it if you kept visiting," he says. "When I get out of the hospital."

I frown. "It's not normal procedure."

"But you will?"

I suck my teeth before nodding. "Yes," I say. "Why not?"

Perhaps it's finding him that does it. What else can explain why, for the first time in years, I don't dream of the zoo. I don't have to watch Dad sit there, tearing his soul apart. I don't have to see it all over again just as I saw it when I was a child, but hardened, embittered by the knowledge I've gained over the years.

How many times have I asked myself the same old questions: might he have stayed, had he known she would never be unfaithful again? Was it his death that made her stop? Why wasn't I enough to keep him alive? And most painfully of all, could I have done anything to save him if only he'd stayed?

But it's different now, knowing I have Ron where I want him. In a few days' time I will be alone with him, just as she was all those years ago.

And his life will be in my hands.

The front door is unlocked so I let myself in, closing it gently behind me and flicking the catch. The house smells of TCP and cigarettes. The fire is dying in the grate.

Ron lies on the sofa, a blanket round him. "So," he says, sounding weary. "Here we are."

I frown. "Are you okay?"

He raises his eyes to meet mine. "Okay?" He laughs. "No. I'm old and I'm lonely. But that's all right," he says. "After all, we both know why you're here."

"Do we?" I ask, my hand still clasped around the bottle in my pocket.

He nods. "You look just like her, Julie," he says, sighing. "I understand. You lost so much. It was wrong, what we did."

I stare at him and for the first time, I wonder what I'm doing there. What I hope to gain. Or what I hope to recover. But I know that this is not the way. I'm worth more than this.

I remove my hand from the medicine bottle, letting it fall deep into my pocket. "Goodbye, Ron," I say, stepping back towards the door.

He nods gently. "Goodbye, Julie," he whispers.

I step out onto the garden path and walk steadily away, not looking back.

Julia Graves

Coming Home

The light in the bookshop was fading when I saw Reggie again. The years had not been kind to him; his complexion was tired, his face lined and what remained of his hair was flecked with grey, but it was unmistakably him.

My first instinct was to duck behind the bookstands, to hide myself from his view, but my legs refused to obey my command and there I stood, exposed, between classic fiction and fantasy, my eyes glued to his familiar face.

There was a moment when he looked up, that he did not appear to recognise me, his expression one of mild irritation. I asked myself then, had I changed so much? Had my recently dyed copper hair disguised me so effectively? Were my curves so much curvier than back then, when he used to run his hands over my body and tell me he knew it even with his eyes closed?

I was surprised to find my reaction closer to disappointment than relief. But then his cool, blue eyes came to life and he smiled a slow, easy smile.

"Annie," he said softly.

It was then I knew I was lost.

Reggie was the only person who called me Annie, though not the only one who ever tried. Occasionally, throughout my childhood, the nickname would escape my father's lips, only to be met with a glare from my mother that would have silenced the most forthright of men.

"Her name is Annette," she would snap, eyes flashing as her needle darted through the fabric of her embroidery. "She's not a poor little orphan, as well you know." He would take up his pipe then and his newspaper, winking at me from behind the pages.

When I met Reggie and started to get to know his friends, it was only natural that they, taking their cue from him, should call me Annie. Then I would blush and, feeling rather embarrassed, gently request that they call me Annette.

By rights, Reggie's family should have lived up to Mother's standards, but he had had a little trouble with the law. "Some unspeakable business with credit cards," Mother sniffed. "I simply can't permit you to continue courting him. Of course, you must understand, dear."

Perhaps I did understand her reasons, but that didn't mean I could adhere to her wishes. And so we continued dating in secret. Sneaking around without my mother's knowledge was deliciously exhilarating. Perhaps that appealed more than the relationship itself, but I was too young to make the distinction.

We were engaged soon afterwards. Reggie insisted on coming to the house to ask Daddy for my hand in marriage, whether to conform with tradition or to flaunt his victory over my mother, I'll never know. I remember watching at the draughty sitting room window as he made his way up the drive, gravel crunching under his confident footsteps. A mixture of excitement and fear gnawed at my stomach as he approached. I ran out into the cold hallway to open the door and ushered him through to the sitting room, where a fire burned dimly in the grate.

I perched on the edge of the familiar, deep sofa, patting the seat next to me, but this was no social visit. Reggie stood to deliver his petition, Mother and Daddy in their matching, high-backed wing chairs resembling, to my wary eyes, a pair of high court judges.

"No! Absolutely not. We simply can't permit it," Mother said, glaring at Reggie.

But this time it was Daddy's turn to silence her with a wave of his hand and a stern look of his own. "Annette," he said gently, drawing my gaze away from the look of fury contorting Mother's face.

"Yes, Daddy?"

"Are you absolutely sure this is what you want?"

"Frederick!" Mother's voice trembled with outrage.

"Elizabeth!" Daddy shot back. It was the first time I had heard him raise his voice to Mother. "It's not your decision," he said, slowly and deliberately. "It's *my* blessing he's come to ask and I'll damn well make up my own mind whether to give it."

I held my breath as Mother scurried from the room with a sob, her white, lacy handkerchief pressed to her mouth. Whether she was crying or simply seeking attention I don't know. Her authority in the household had never been challenged before. Seeing her laid so low felt like a long-overdue victory, for a brief moment, at least.

It was the last time I ever saw her.

"Reginald Hunter Squires," I said slowly, drinking in his familiar face, savouring the name I had not spoken for so long.

"Annette Lucinda Masterson," he said, his eyes not leaving mine.

"Squires," I said gently. "Annette Lucinda Squires."

"You didn't change it."

I shook my head, my eyes tracing the lines on his face, studying it intently to distinguish the old from the new.

"How are things with you?" I said, unwilling to let him turn and walk back out of my life again so soon.

"Good." He nodded. "Great." He paused, looking over his shoulder, as if noticing for the first time the clank of cups and the swoosh of the coffee machine in the corner. "Drink?" he said, and I dared to imagine I detected a hint of hopefulness in his tone.

I hesitated. "Okay." I looked over at the coffee shop, at the earnestness of the students poring over their books. "But not here."

He nodded and smiled. "Let me pay for this, then," he said, indicating the crime novel in his hand.

The realities of married life came as something of a shock. I had never had to worry about money before. My parents had given me a more than ample allowance, and had I ever wanted for anything, Daddy would buy it for me.

"Frederick!" Mother would chastise him sometimes. "You'll spoil the child."

"Shh, Elizabeth," he would reply. "It's not like we're short."

Now the allowance had stopped, cut off absolutely and irrevocably. Mother refused to see me, and Daddy could no longer subsidise my lifestyle, relying as he did on her family's legacy.

"She's cut my allowance, too," he said miserably, passing me his last five-pound note as he sipped his coffee from our least chipped mug. "I can barely afford to buy a round of drinks at the golf club any longer. The chaps must think it most peculiar."

I rubbed the note between my fingers, hoping a second would magically reveal itself. When it did not, I reluctantly pressed it back into his hand. "I can't take this, Daddy." But heaven knows I could have used it.

After our marriage, I had come to realise that Reggie's income, gained here and there in deals of varying legitimacy, was sporadic at best. Suddenly, I had been faced with rent and bills to pay and had been forced to take on a job as receptionist at a doctor's surgery. Again, Daddy had come to my rescue, setting me up for an interview with one of his golf club friends.

Looking around the waiting room at the girls with their portfolios, I knew at once that I was the least experienced and probably the least qualified candidate for the job, and yet somehow I was offered the position. I would have loved to have turned it down on principle, but pride had to take a back seat to necessity.

All the same, my salary was barely enough to cover the rent on our cosy one-bedroom flat and the food. It was a struggle to pay the bills and there was nothing left for luxuries, no allowance for clothes, no money for paint to brighten the drab walls or rugs to hide the thin patches in the carpet.

"Let's go to the cinema," Reggie would say, but when we got there, he would discover that he had forgotten his wallet and I would be forced to purchase the tickets from the money I had been saving to pay for electricity or gas. Soon we stopped going out at all.

Reggie meanwhile would borrow money from me. "Just for a few days, babe," he would say. "I need to fill the car up. I'll pay you back next week, when the money comes in." But somehow, he never did.

One day I got home from the surgery to find Reggie waiting for me, bottle of champagne in hand, a huge bunch of flowers in a new crystal vase looking ridiculously out of place on the old formica table. I swallowed my annoyance at the expense and plastered a smile on my face.

"Good news, Annie." Reggie grinned. "I've got a job."

"A job?" Reggie had never had a job in his life, not in the conventional sense. "What kind of a job?"

"Babe!" Reggie sounded hurt, but not for long. "The kind of job that means we won't have to worry about money any more," he said, picking me up and twirling me in the air.

"Really?"

"Really. You can quit the doc's just as soon as you like." He swung me back down onto my feet and his grin was infectious. "Our money worries are over, Annie." And he took my face in his hands and kissed me, long and hard. I swallowed my annoyance and my anxiety and allowed myself to be swept along on the wave of his enthusiasm.

The only problem with Reggie's new employment, it became apparent, was that it took Reggie away for long periods at a time. It started off as a few days each month. "We're setting up a new warehouse," he told me. "Expanding, Annie. Soon be done and dusted." But before long he was leaving me for two weeks, three weeks or even a month and when he came home it was never for more than a few days at a time. The business, it seemed, needed him more than me.

I carried on working at the surgery, but money was no longer my aim: the contributions Reggie sent home were more than enough to cover my, by now, meagre needs. No, it was companionship I was seeking.

"Where to?" Reggie said, tucking his book inside his neat, brown woollen jacket as he joined me at the door.

I looked up and down the bustling high street, glanced at my watch. Shopkeepers were starting to carry in their wares. The cafés would be closing and I preferred to avoid the enforced sociability of a pub. "Surprise me."

He paused for a moment, a thoughtful look on his face. Then with a grin, he set off at a march. "Come on, Annie," he said, taking my hand in his. "I know just the place."

Whenever Reggie came home to me, he seemed preoccupied.

"Give up the job," I urged him. "You've earned plenty to keep us going for now." But he wouldn't hear of it.

Meanwhile, he was growing anxious for a child. "About time you had a baby," he said repeatedly. "Reggie Junior. Your looks and my brains, what a combination!"

"Patience, Reggie," I would urge him. "We'll have a baby when the time is right." But secretly I was worried that the time would never be right. It was true that he spent long periods away, but we had long since given up using birth control and still nothing had happened.

"Don't worry, Annie," Reggie reassured me. "You're too tense, too stressed. That's probably what's stopping you from getting pregnant. You should give up work, relax."

Eventually, I gave in to pressure and quit my job. But far from being the answer to all my problems, it seemed to exacerbate them. Now I found myself at home alone full time, with no one but my father, on his occasional visits, for company.

I worried about Reggie, about the long hours he was working and how his work seemed to drain him.

Secretly, I worried about what he was doing, how he was coming by his income, but I didn't dare confront him for fear of destroying what remained of our relationship.

In the end, when the knock on the door came, it was not a policeman who stood outside, but a mousy young lady, a child in her arms, her round belly indicating the imminent arrival of another.

"Mrs Squires?" she said nervously from beneath the hood of her brown duffel coat. She spoke with a Midlands accent, curious in these parts. I wondered what had brought her so far from home.

I nodded. "That's me. And you are?"

She shuffled uncomfortably. "I'm also Mrs Squires."

I inclined my head, frowning in confusion. Reggie didn't have any siblings and the last we had heard of his father, he was off shooting antelope in Africa, not bedding young ladies in the Midlands.

"I don't understand..." I said, although a dull comprehension was gnawing at the edges of my consciousness.

The child in her arms yawned and buried his face in her shoulder. The girl, not much more than a child herself, looked exhausted too. "Can I..." She looked up at me, blinking urgently. "Can I come in?"

I nodded and held the door open for her to pass through.

The streetlights flickered on as we walked the damp streets, their light reflected in the puddles on the pavements. My heart gave a skip when Reggie stopped outside an elegant townhouse, slipped a key into the lock and held the door open for me to step inside.

"You live here?" I said, taking in the masculine scent of the place, all leather and oak with a hint of cigar smoke.

He nodded. "Couldn't stay away from my roots forever."

"Alone?"

He inclined his head, smiled slightly. "Yes, Annie," he said softly. "Alone." He held his hand out, indicating the stairs and chuckled at the look of astonishment on my face. "Coffee," he said. "The kitchen's right this way."

Climbing the stairs behind him, I paused, seeking any hint of feminine presence but there was none, except perhaps the tidiness of the place.

"Mrs McIntyre," he said, as if reading my thoughts. "Theresa. Comes in once a week, Tuesdays. Cleans the place a treat. Unfortunately," he waved a hand toward the stack of plates next to the sink, "the same can't be said for me."

I smiled and walked over to the kitchen window, looking out onto the street and the park opposite. The leaves on the trees were just starting to turn, creating a kaleidoscope of red, brown and amber. Children ran between them looking for conkers, which they stuffed into their bulging pockets.

"I've missed you Annie," Reggie said, coming up behind me and slipping his arms easily around my waist. I could smell his old, familiar aftershave and shut my eyes, breathing in his masculinity, peeling back the layers of my mind.

"I've missed you, too," I said.

He turned me to face him then, pulling me to him and kissing me hungrily. My legs felt unsteady as he gently led me by the hand, past the gurgling coffee machine, out of the kitchen, up another flight of stairs and into his bedroom.

"Welcome home," he murmured, pulling me down onto the bed.

I felt drained after the other Mrs Squires had left. I hadn't asked her first name and she hadn't asked mine. We were rivals, but our situation had also made us comrades.

"What shall we do?" she had asked me, her thin, pale face drawn. "We could call the police?"

But we both knew that calling the police could have unintended consequences. Start digging into Reggie's affairs and who knew what they might uncover. Instead, we agreed to face him together. She had taken the train back home and I would follow in the morning.

"How did you find me?" I said as she stood on the doorstep, child in her arms, ready to leave.

"Bank statements," she said simply, with a tight little laugh. "Money."

The train journey up to the Midlands was long and uncomfortable, although the discomfort came as much from the knowledge of what I was about to face as the rickety carriage in which I travelled.

I disembarked at Derby and took a taxi to the house, wishing to retain my composure for the ordeal to come.

It was a handsome semi-detached house, with pebble-dashed walls and sash windows. My mother, I knew, would have despised living in such a house but, to me, the space it afforded, the large tidy lawn out the front and the apple tree, branches laden with fruit, made it the ideal family home. Did he own it? I wondered, enviously. Had he provided a proper home for his second wife and child, while I still lived in a tiny, rented flat?

When the second Mrs Squires opened the solid, wooden door, she acknowledged my presence with a tight smile and a nod, but did not speak as I stepped through the door and into the warm, dimly-lit hallway. I knew at once that he was there.

"Come here, Charlie, son," I heard his familiar, deep voice say.

I craned my neck to see around the living room door and watched the image reflected in the mirror above the mantelpiece. There he was: my husband, his child in his arms. My heart ached that I had been too slow to provide him with a family of our own, that he had had to look elsewhere to find fulfilment as a father. And yet a rage burned deep inside, with myself for my stupidity, my wilful blindness as much as with him for his arrogance, deceit and betrayal.

The boy saw me before Reggie did. "Who are you?" he said, his thin eyebrows pulled together in a tight frown.

I swallowed, stepped into the room, and tried to smile. "Hello," I said. "I'm here to see your father."

"Daddy?" the boy looked up at Reggie, who set him down onto the floor and stood, a look of astonishment on his face.

"Annie," he said, helplessly. He looked from me to the girl behind me, opening his mouth to speak again, but no further sound came out and he sat heavily back down on the sofa.

"Don't worry, Reggie, I won't stay long," I said in as business-like a tone as I could muster. "I've just brought your things."

I waved a hand towards the hallway, indicating the large suitcase into which I had packed all of his belongings. "You needn't come back to collect anything. It's all there."

He stared at me uncomprehending, then, again, his eyes drifted to his other wife, seeming to plead with her.

She bent to pick up her child, hugging him tight against her, the tears rolling down her face. "No," she said simply. "It's over, Reggie."

I don't know what happened after that, whether he collected his belongings meekly and left, tail between his legs. I can't imagine he did, not Reggie. And yet I don't want to think about him begging her to let him stay. I imagined him out in the cold, forced to make a new start. From two wives to none. But I don't know for sure.

I had half expected him to come back to me, to beg me to let him stay, had feared and longed for it in equal measure. But that didn't happen. I never saw him again.

Until now.

Reggie was as tender a lover as I had remembered. Afterwards he brought me coffee and scones in bed, laughing at the look of horror on my face.

"What?" he said. "You think that after what we've just done to these sheets a few crumbs are going to make a difference?"

I pulled a face, but secretly I revelled in the indulgence and in being close to him again. We chatted as we ate, about old times, about our lives, but I noticed that he avoided any mention of his other family and so did I.

"Annie, we've got so much catching up to do!" Reggie said, his blue eyes dancing brightly. "And then there's my club, you must come. They'll love you. I'm so glad we've got another chance." He pulled me to him, stroking my hair, his voice dropping to a murmur. "You were always the one."

I smiled, enjoying the warmth of his body, indulging in the fantasy of being Reggie's sidekick again. But we both knew it was nothing more than that: a fantasy.

We made love once more before Reggie fell asleep. I watched him briefly, the way the moonlight falling on his face turned back the years and made him look young again. Then I dressed and sneaked from the room as quietly as I could, shutting the door behind me.

It was dark when I stepped into my hotel room, but for the dull glow from the laptop balanced on the edge of the low coffee table. I leaned against the door and sighed heavily, releasing the tension from my body, letting go of a lifetime of regrets. It was time to move on.

Gently, I perched on the arm of the sofa, tucking a blanket lightly around the tall frame of the boy who lay curled up, asleep on the deep cushions.

Tomorrow he would ask me where I had been, why I hadn't turned up for dinner at the tiny retirement flat his grandpa now called home. His blue eyes, so like his father's, would study my face as I struggled to reply. I would not - *could* not - tell him the truth, not after all these years.

I would repeat the lie to Daddy when he picked us up to drive us to the airport, but he would read the truth in my face even as I begged him to join us on the flight, even as he insisted he was too old for new horizons.

Tomorrow, we would return home to Colorado, my son and I.

Julia Graves

Thank You

Joanna and the Black Dog Writing Group for
encouraging me to write my first short stories

David for giving me the confidence to edit and
publish this collection

Kimberly for being my first reader
and most enthusiastic supporter

Jodie and Daniel for your support and
encouragement throughout the editing process

and, of course, my family in the UK.

About the Author

Julia Graves is a writer and language teacher.

She spent her childhood in Chelmsford, Essex and later studied Modern Languages at the University of Bradford, with placements in Paris and León.

She is now happily settled in Valencia, Spain. You can read her blog about her experiences in and around the city at vivalencia.me